Dea

Harleqin ...
in 2009 with an entire year's worth of special
programs showcasing the talent and variety
that have made us the world's leading romance
publisher.

With this collection of vintage novels, we are
thrilled to be able to journey with you to the roots
of our success: six books that hark back to the
very earliest days of our history, when the fare was
decidedly adventurous, often mysterious and full of
passion—1950s-style!

It is such fun to be able to present these works
with their original text and cover art, which we
hope both current readers and collectors of popular
fiction will find entertaining.

Thank you for helping us to achieve and celebrate
this milestone!

Warmly,

Donna Hayes,
Publisher and CEO

# The Harlequin Story

To millions of readers around the world, Harlequin and romance fiction are synonymous. With a publishing record of 120 titles a month in 29 languages in 107 international markets on 6 continents, there is no question of Harlequin's success.

But like all good stories, Harlequin's has had some twists and turns.

In 1949, Harlequin was founded in Winnipeg, Canada. In the beginning, the company published a wide range of books—including the likes of Agatha Christie, Sir Arthur Conan Doyle, James Hadley Chase and Somerset Maugham—all for the low price of twenty-five cents.

By the mid 1950s, Richard Bonnycastle was in complete control of the company, and at the urging of his wife—and chief editor—began publishing the romances of British firm Mills & Boon. The books sold so well that Harlequin eventually bought Mills & Boon outright in 1971.

In 1970, Harlequin expanded its distribution into the U.S. and contracted its first American author so that it could offer the first truly American romances. By 1980, that concept became a full-fledged series called Harlequin Superromance, the first romance line to originate outside the U.K.

The 1980s saw continued growth into global markets as well as the purchase of American publisher, Silhouette Books. By 1992, Harlequin dominated the genre, and ten years later was publishing more than half of all romances released in North America.

Now in our sixtieth anniversary year, Harlequin remains true to its history of being *the* romance publisher, while constantly creating innovative ways to deliver variety in what women want to read. And as we forge ahead into other types of fiction and nonfiction, we are always mindful of the hallmark of our success over the past six decades—guaranteed entertainment!

# KISS YOUR ELBOW

## ALAN HANDLEY

HARLEQUIN®

TORONTO • NEW YORK • LONDON
AMSTERDAM • PARIS • SYDNEY • HAMBURG
STOCKHOLM • ATHENS • TOKYO • MILAN • MADRID
PRAGUE • WARSAW • BUDAPEST • AUCKLAND

Recycling programs
for this product may
not exist in your area.

ISBN-13: 978-0-373-83745-8

KISS YOUR ELBOW

www.eHarlequin.com

**Printed in U.S.A.**

## ALAN HANDLEY

Emmy® Award-winning director Alan Handley had a celebrated career on stage and in television that spanned thirty years. He started off as a stage actor in the 1930s before moving into directing and producing shows such as *The Dinah Shore Show*. He won an Emmy® for directing a Julie Andrews special in 1965. He passed away in January 1990 at the age of 77.

# CHAPTER ONE

I WAS IN BED—WHICH IS WHERE I usually am at ten o'clock in the morning—when the phone rang.

"What's with you? This is Nellie." As though it was necessary to tell me who it was with that croak for a voice, even if she did wake me up. I lit a cigarette because she liked to talk for a long time and so do I and she was paying for the call and I didn't have anything else to do.

"I'm still in bed."

"Well, do you think you could get that long lean brownness the hell out of that bed for a job?"

"How much? It's a nice bed."

"Twenty-five a day for maybe three days or more. Of course, if you're not interested, I got a book full of youth and beauty right here at my elbow."

"If it's more of those smoker pictures, the answer is no."

"Now, Timmy, darling, you know that wasn't my fault. They told me that short was only for advertising purposes. Besides, the money was good."

"Well, I don't need that kind of advertising yet. What's the gag this time?"

"Can you be in my office in an hour?"

"Tell me now."

"I tell you nothing till you sign Nellie's little receipt book. Do you or don't you?"

"Make it an hour and a half?"

"Who's there with you?"

"Nobody," I said. "And besides, what's it to you?"

"If there's nobody there, you can make it in an hour. Eleven sharp. Those are my last words." And she banged up the receiver.

Twenty-five bucks a day for three days…that must be a picture…maybe I can get a close-up…be nice to the cameraman and the assistant director…one good close-up…who knows what might happen? Once more into the breach, dear friends…

So I got up, showered and started to get dressed. Thank God I had a clean shirt and my suit had just been pressed, because for twenty-five bucks a day, no matter what tricks Nellie was cooking up for me, I had to be good. I got into my gray double-breasted, which is one of my two answers to a couple of my more unkind friends that I have got another suit besides a dinner jacket. I did look through the pockets of my evening clothes to see how much money I had. There was nine dollars and some change together with match folders from the Barberry Room, the Stork and the Ruban Bleu. Diana, the woman I'd been out with last night, and I had certainly been on the town. I had to get this job of Nellie's or I was going to be very, very hungry in a couple of days.

I put the money in my pocket and the folders in the

bureau drawer where I save the ones from the tonier places. It sometimes impresses people when you're trying to get a job if you pull out one from the Stork or "21." I finished dressing and put on my coat and hat and went out.

The rooming house where I live was nicknamed the Casbah by one of the inmates after seeing that Boyer movie a long time ago and the name stuck. It's just off, but not quite far enough off, Sheridan Square and on Saturday nights when the visiting firemen make a tour of Greenwich Village—which usually means Jimmy Kelly's or a couple of the joints on Fourth Street—we get the usual drunks being sick in the vestibule or ringing the bell and asking for Marge. The Casbah like most rooming houses usually has a couple of transient Marges in spite of the professional jealousy of Helga who runs it, but on a Saturday night the Marges can pick their own drunks.

In the hall I ran into Kendall Thayer, who promptly hit me for a couple of bucks and I, like a dope, let him have them.

Whenever I get really depressed, which isn't often because I have a lot of little tricks worked out to keep it from happening, I think of Kendall Thayer. He's a but-for-the-grace-of-God-there-I-go lad. He's me in cornstarch. Years ago he was a very famous silent picture leading man with a swimming pool and the works, but the bottle moved in and the works moved out, and now he's ended up just another lush in the smallest and cheapest room in the Casbah, and, believe me, that's small and cheap.

Like the rest of us, he feels that a break is just around the corner, the break that will get him another movie contract and put him right back up there. After all, he says, C. Aubrey Smith and Edmund Gwenn can't live forever, just as I say that Tyrone Power and Hank Fonda and Gregory Peck weren't born on a movie set, and people lent them dimes to eat in their day, too.

Kendall manages to get odd jobs once in a while with radio audience-participation shows where they have plants in the studio. He usually gets five bucks a throw and six cakes of soap or a carton of breakfast food, which he tries to peddle to other people in the Casbah, but recently business has been off all over town.

"You going out, Tim?" he asked me.

"Yeah, got a call," I said, dealing him out the two dollars. That left me seven.

"Going to be out long?"

"I don't know. Hope it's for a job. Why?"

"I was just wondering if you'd let me have the key to your door. I left your phone number and I'm expecting a call and it's rather important. I'd prefer it didn't come over the house phone." I could understand that because the only phone besides mine in the Casbah is out in the hall and everybody knows what is said over it even before the person talking.

So I said, "Sure. Here's the key, but don't mess with my studs and cuff links." He gave me what, I am sure, back in the silent days was famous as his rueful smile, and I went on downstairs and out on the street.

I stopped at the Riker's on the corner of Sheridan

Square for orange juice and coffee and went down the subway hole at exactly ten forty-five.

I took the uptown local to Fourteenth Street and closed my eyes and prayed. If there's one thing that's going to drive me nuts quicker than anything else, it's living on a local subway stop.

I used to be able to treat it as a game. But now I've gotten superstitious about it. It's become an omen, and can wreck my whole day.

If, when I get to Fourteenth Street, which is an express stop, and the express is waiting right there…it's a red-letter day. Then all I have to do is run across the platform and there I am at Times Square in two stops. But when the local pulls in and there isn't an express there, I start quietly blowing my top. It's ridiculous, I know, but so is the superstition about whistling in dressing rooms or saying the last line of a play in rehearsal. I don't suppose I make or lose two minutes either way, but this subway business when it doesn't work out right is the black cat across my path, or the broken mirror. And today when I decide I'll take a chance and change to an express, it gets lost over in Brooklyn or someplace and I know of two locals, at least, that beat me to Times Square. That was a sure sign that today was going to be a *not* day and I should have stayed in bed.

I got to Times Square nervous and mad and feeling like saying to hell with Nellie and going over to one of the flea-bag movies on Forty-second Street and giving my evil omens time to cool off. I would have, too, except that I had just seven bucks in the whole world, and twenty-five bucks is twenty-five bucks.

So I walked up Times Square past the Paramount Theater Building—which when I first came to New York was considered a cathedral of the motion picture or something, but is now just where high school kids play hookey with name bands. And then on the corner of Forty-fourth Street, which I had to pass to get to the Shubert Building and Nellie's office, was Walgreen's Drug Store.

When you're in grammar school, there's always a Sweet Shop or Pete's where you go after school and hang around. In prep school or high school there's the Jigger Shop or Joe's or Ye Sweete Shoppe, and in college there's the Den or Mike's, so you might know that when you enroll in the theater there would be some hangouts, too. There are, and one of them is Walgreen's Drug Store. And it's the first rung on the ladder. When you get a little bit better jobs you start dropping in at Sardi's, and then, maybe the first time you get billing, it's "21" and Toots Shor's or the Stork or Morocco, and when you're tops it's the Colony at the right table.

Anyhow, here's Walgreen's. I guess it's a good idea having a place like that. Trying to get ahead in the theater is a lonely business and any opportunity to huddle in groups is gratefully received. But I didn't have time to huddle this morning.

The little bar in Sardi's restaurant was empty except for the bartender polishing glasses. After all, eleven o'clock is a little early even for actors to start in—except the ones that can't get out of bed without brushing their teeth with a belt of gin, and they were still in bed... belting away.

Nellie's alleged office is across the street from Sardi's in the Shubert Building, and Nick Stein with a couple of polo-coated singers was already in the elevator when I got on. Nick's an assistant press agent and runs a syndicated gossip column in a lot of out-of-town newspapers. I give him tips once in a while, and he mentions me once in a while and also gives me ducats for shows he's handling, which are useful for paying back obligations and, sometimes, you can even sell them.

"What's with you, Tim?" Nick asked me. "Get any items? Did you make the rounds last night?"

"Yeah," I said. "When I think of the ulcers I save you..." I told him one I'd heard about the Broadway producer who'd been clipped for plenty by three previous wives, so now, every time he gave his current wife a present he actually insisted she sign a paper saying it was hers only so long as she was married to him. "How's that?"

"Not bad. Stop by the office with me, and I'll fix you up for a show tonight." So I rode up to the tenth floor, and Nick gave me three seats to one of his frantic flops one jump ahead of the stop clause.

Coming back to the hall with the tickets, the indicator said both elevators were on the ground floor, so it was quicker to walk down to Nellie's office. Somebody else was on the stairs a couple of flights below me. I couldn't see who it was though I could hear shoes clanging on iron treads. Whoever it was seemed to be in an awful hurry.

Nellie's roost consists of two connecting cubicles at the end of the dark corridor. Waiting actors are the only ones that ever use the tiny front room, except when Henry Frobisher is producing a play and then Nellie gets grand and installs a secretary who is usually some unemployed actor working for peanuts on the chance that Nellie will get him a job with Frobisher, which, of course, she never does.

The first room was empty when I opened the door and walked in, which wasn't unusual because most people who make the rounds have learned that Nellie doesn't show till after lunch unless she's very busy and that's practically never. By waving aside the stale cigarette smoke laced with gin that hung from the ceiling like portieres, I could make out Nellie leaning over her desk and I started to walk back to her.

I guess I must have said something silly, like "Boo! you pretty creature." I usually do, but it didn't make any difference whether I did or not because Nellie didn't hear me. Nellie couldn't hear me. Nellie was dead.

## CHAPTER TWO

I JUST STOOD THERE STARING at her. She was flopped
across her desk and had filed herself about as neatly as
anything else in that rats' nest on her old-fashioned
country editor-type filing spindle. I could see the heavy
wrought-iron base of the spindle jutting out around the
edges of her right breast. There wasn't much blood, which
is probably the reason I didn't start heaving, because in
the army I developed sort of a thing about blood.

Nellie alive and kicking is nobody's dream girl. She's
a chiseler, an agent, a sharpie with a shady buck. She's
fat and sloppy and although she undoubtedly owns
another dress, I don't remember ever seeing her in any
but this mottled grayish-green job which bitchy actors
are apt to swear stopped being a dress years ago and now
just grows on her like moss. But all the same, I was kind
of fond of her.

I felt for her pulse, which wasn't—and that's all. I've
done enough of those where-were-you-on-the-night-of
bills in summer stock to know better than to start
juggling bodies around now.

Lying open and almost hidden under one pudgy arm

and doing its bit toward helping her hair sop up the blood was Nellie's Youth and Beauty Book, which was, besides the phone and spindle, all of Nellie's office equipment. In it she kept all the names of actors and producers she knew, listed her appointments and stuffed it full of letters and bills. She must have had it refilled every year because it always had the same tooled leather cover.

Falling into the old first-act routine, I slid the book out from under her arm and looked at the page for today. As I figured, my name was down for an eleven o'clock appointment. There were three other entries ahead of mine. One I knew very well: Maggie Lanson. She was to be there at eleven, too. Nellie was supposed to have been at Chez Ernest, the chi-chi dress place at ten. The other name I couldn't recognize. There were just initials for the last name. It was Bobby LeB. and he had an appointment for ten-thirty. That was all for the morning, but in the afternoon she was to see Henry Frobisher at his office at three-thirty, and she had a dinner date with a little ingenue around town I knew, as who didn't, named Libby Drew.

Suddenly the phone rang. That was the cue for me to start blowing up in my scene and almost closed me before I opened. I had moved the corpus—at least the arm—when I pulled out the book, and I didn't want to get in any jam. My name was in that book and there was nobody around to knock some sense into me, and the damned phone kept ringing and ringing and I couldn't bring myself to answer it. Suddenly I got a load of a scene behind a gauze scrim I didn't want any part of—

me sweating under a lot of blinding lights with all the Irish character actors in town waving rubber hoses at me and shouting, "Who done it, Runch?" and me not being able to tell them. When I play that scene I want to have a few of the toppers.

Then the montage began. You know, lots of presses running and front pages flying at you like bats out of hell and banner heads screaming "Actor Slays Agent" and "Fiend Convicted." If only the phone had stopped that ringing or I had stopped that nonsense of thinking I was playing the lead in some crappy whodunit at the Rialto and done what I should have done, everything would have been all right. At least for me. But no... Once a ham always a ham. So I picked up the Youth and Beauty Book and stuck it under my coat—still like in reel two—and copped a sneak.

The hall was empty. I had another brain wave and walked back up to the tenth floor and got on the elevator there and rode down. The only stop was the fifth floor where two polo coats got back on.

I did a walk-not-run out onto Forty-fourth and aimed west. I didn't want to pass Sardi's or Walgreen's again because by this time I had worked myself up to such a point that if somebody had said Boo! to me, I'd have waved aside the black mask and asked for that final cigarette.

## CHAPTER THREE

I WALKED UP EIGHTH AVENUE for a couple of blocks trying to decide what to do. The Forty-second Street fleabags didn't seem to solve anything, though in all the books, ticket stubs seem to be wonderful alibis—except that the people that use them for alibis always seem to end up in the last chapter behind the eight ball. Which is where it looked like I was going to end up without costing me forty cents, either. Of course, I shouldn't have taken the Youth and Beauty Book.

And then I thought of Maggie Lanson. Even if her name hadn't been in the book for an eleven o'clock appointment, sooner or later I would have thought of Maggie Lanson. She is the only other person I know of in the world that feels the same way I do about most things. We are, as she is wont to say after a couple of slugs of pernod, *sympatique.*

She's exactly my age, thirty-two, and was terribly pretty about ten years ago but the pernod hasn't helped that part of it much. She's quite rich, mostly from an early husband she divorced about seven years ago, and she tries to be an actress when she thinks of it. That was

how I first met her. We were in the same show, my one
hit, for six months right after her divorce. I guess she
felt she had to have something to do nights.

I don't know if I thought she would be able to tell me
who had done Nellie in. Maybe she was early for her
appointment or maybe she didn't keep it at all—which
wouldn't be unusual. And if she did maybe she knew
this Bobby LeB. She knew the most alarming collection
of people. Anyway, Maggie was the only person in the
world I wanted to see.

Her apartment, at the corner of Fifth Avenue and one
of the Sixties, is on the fifth floor, and there is a buzzer
system and a work-it-yourself elevator. I had a key
because she didn't mind my dropping in if I was in the
neighborhood—whether she was there or not—provided
I called up first and emptied the ash trays when I left. I
dialed her number in the corner drugstore (only in that
section of town they are called "chemists" or "apothe-
caries") before walking over, but there wasn't any answer
so I went up to her apartment and let myself in.

It's a nice apartment if you don't mind stripes.
Mostly gray and yellow stripes and lots of flowers. But
the chairs are comfortable and the Capehart works and
there's generally plenty to drink. A big living room with
a practical fireplace, a foyer, bedroom and bath and a
minute kitchenette in which ice cubes are the only thing
she knows the recipe for. I poured myself a mahogany
Scotch because by this time it was two minutes after
twelve, which made it legal as far as I'm concerned.
Then I sat down and started thinking about how soon

what had happened was going to hit me and what a jerk
I was not to leave that damn book in Nellie's office and
call the cops. I took out the Youth and Beauty Book. The
blood had dried on its edges, and on the page that had
been open were a few squiggles in an unpleasant shade
of brown that had been painted with Nellie's own
blood—her hair having been the paintbrush—when I
pulled it out from under her.

It was a sort of hammering with a couple of low moans
thrown in, all kind of muffled. It would go on for a
minute, then stop for a few, then start again. At first I
thought it was only that I should have watered my drink,
but when it came the third time I knew it wasn't the
Scotch and it wasn't me—it was in Maggie's bathroom.
So I got brave by finishing off the Scotch and, making
with a bookend, walked over to the bathroom door.

As I was in this far, I might as well shoot the works.
I grabbed the bookend even tighter and started to open
the bathroom door, only there wasn't any doorknob. It
was lying on the floor right by the door. I picked it up
and fit the square rod in the hole as quietly as I could,
which wasn't very, since I was holding the bookend at
the same time. Softly I turned it and threw open the door.

There was Maggie, nothing on but a nightgown,
lying on the bathroom floor with her chin in one hand
and languidly pounding on the pipes under the wash
basin with a big empty mouthwash bottle in the other.
She looked up from her pounding and after reeling in
her eyes, she recognized me.

"Angel," she said, "for God's sake bring me a drink." She tossed the bottle in a corner where it shattered around a couple of times then lay still. I walked over to help her. My shoes crunched broken glass on the tile floor. "What happened to you?" I helped her to sit up. She yelped and, rolling over on one hip, looked at her behind. Blood was staining her sheer nightgown.

"Now isn't that maddening? A brand-new one, too. Well, don't just stand there, darling. Get me out of here." I picked her up, carried her into the bedroom and deposited her gently, stomach down, on the bed. The cut wasn't very deep, but was bleeding quite a lot. I gave her a face towel to hold on it while I ransacked the medicine cabinet.

"It was that damned doorknob coming off. I've been trapped in there for hours. I broke a couple of bottles pounding on the pipes, but no one would come. If you're expecting to find bandages in that thing you're wasting your time.... There's nothing but sleeping pills." She was right. "Call the superintendent. He's very sweet. I don't think it's worth quite all this fuss, though I'm glad you came in when you did. I was running out of bottles. What about that drink?" I came back to the bed.

"Maggie, how drunk are you?"

"I'm not drunk, Timmy. Honestly I'm not. Well, maybe a little hungover, but I was in there for over two hours, and I do think I should be allowed to be just a little testy, if I want."

"Can you grapple with a horrid fact?"

"Couldn't it wait till I got bandaged up and had a real drink? It'll keep that long, won't it?"

"Yes. I think it'll keep that long." I phoned the super-intendent on the little house phone, and he promptly brought bandages, Mercurochrome and a screwdriver.

He was most apologetic and fixed the doorknob in a few minutes. He could have done it even quicker if he had kept his eyes on his work instead of Maggie, who was still on the bed covered with a blanket trying to negotiate, while lying on her stomach, the drink I had mixed for her. I finally got him out and left Maggie to fix the bandage by herself and started pacing back and forth in the living room.

The cut wasn't at all serious, but I was still a little queasy from it. Bleeding women, two in the same hour, were rapidly getting me down.

Maggie finally came out of the bedroom dressed in a blue housecoat with more stripes and brushing her hair.

"I know I'm stuck with that adhesive tape for the rest of my life. I used practically the whole roll."

"At least you've got a cast-iron alibi."

"Whatever should I want an alibi for?"

"Did you have any appointments this morning?"

The brush stopped in midair. "Oh my God, Nellie! I forgot all about it. She called yesterday and told me to come in this morning for a job. I'd better phone her."

"You needn't bother. She's been murdered."

"What a pity. Oh, well, I don't suppose I'd have gotten the job anyway."

"Maggie, I said that Nellie's been murdered."

"I heard you, dear. And about time, too, if you ask me."

"What makes you say that?"

"But, angel...she's an *agent*."

"Maybe so, but sooner or later the police are going to want to know who killed her."

"What are you getting in such a tizzy about? It isn't anybody we know, is it?"

"Maybe it is."

"Oh, good. Who? Tell me."

"I thought perhaps you'd know something about it. That's why I came here this morning."

"Believe me, Timmy, I've got something better to do than go around murdering Nellie Brant. I think I will now have another drink. No, you stay here, I'll get them this time. Since I can't sit down, I might as well be busy." She went into the foyer to the bar and brought us back a couple of straight Scotches. "Would you like to play Gin Rummy? We could do it on the mantelpiece."

"No, I would not like to play Gin Rummy. Please, Maggie, I'm serious."

"I'm sorry, Timmy. I do mean to listen but that affair with the bathroom has made me rather jumpy. I wish I could sit down." She pulled some pillows from the couch and lined them up on the floor and lay on her stomach. "There, that's much better. Now tell me everything in one word."

"Well, Nellie called me up this morning and..."

"What time was that?"

"About ten o'clock, I think."

"And she was dead when you saw her, whenever it

was? As a matter of fact, I don't imagine she was dead at all. Probably drunk. She's a notorious nipper."

"She was dead, all right. I took her pulse. She was still warm, but definitely dead."

"Oh, but that doesn't mean a thing. I'm forever reading about people with no pulse at all carrying on like mad. I read about a chicken with his head chopped completely off, mind you, living to a ripe old age."

I didn't like it one bit that my big moment did not turn out to be a big moment after all. And besides, I *knew* Nellie was dead. The picture of that body kept coming into focus in spite of the Scotch. I kept fighting it, trying to make it vague and blurry again, but it didn't work. I lay down on the floor beside Maggie and stared up at the ceiling.

"Here, lift up your head a minute." I lifted up my head and she pushed a pillow under it. "Now lie back." She stroked my forehead. Her hand was cool. It felt good. "Now then, tell me all. She called you at ten and then what happened?"

I told her exactly what had happened, or at least as near as I could remember. She thought it over for a moment.

"What about fingerprints? They're very smart this season."

"I had my gloves on," I said. I was rather pleased with myself not to be caught with that one.

"Pretty damned clever, aren't you, to…"

"Actually, I didn't really plan it that way," I said. "It just happened."

"…to be able to take a pulse with your gloves on."

She finished on what I thought was an unnecessarily triumphant note.

And, of course, I must have taken my gloves off to feel for Nellie's pulse. I admitted that rather sheepishly.

"And did you put your gloves back on right after you picked up the Youth and Beauty Book?" I couldn't remember. "And did you close the door after you left?" Yes, I was positive of that. "Well, then, you have probably left a print large as life and twice as natural on the office door." I tried desperately to remember if I had put my gloves back on or not.

"But what if I did," I said defensively. "They won't necessarily know whose they are. I'm not in the rogues' gallery—yet."

Maggie regarded me with what I can only describe as a pitying expression.

"Well, what's wrong now?"

"But you were in the army, weren't you? You can remember *that* much, can't you?" After four years of that production you're not liable to forget it in a hurry, and I told her so. "Remember that little card you had to carry about with you that had that repulsive picture of you on it... I could never understand why you didn't go to a really good photographer...."

"So what? I didn't leave my, what you describe as 'repulsive,' portrait on the doorknob, did I?"

"You might just as well have. In case you don't recall, your fingerprints were on that card, too, with a copy probably crouching somewhere in a Washington filing cabinet, with your repulsive portrait on the same page, waiting for just this moment."

I got up and walked over to the window and looked down on Fifth Avenue. It was all crawling and busy and it wasn't raining and it wasn't snowing and it looked fine. Central Park was pleasant, too, even for February. It looked like I would like to keep on seeing it for quite a while yet, but the odds at the moment were less than even.

"Well, I suppose I ought to save the taxpayers some money and give myself up before they go to all that trouble and expense of spreading a dragnet to apprehend the fiend. A flock of New York's Finest are no doubt right this minute combing the Casbah from top to bottom."

Maggie gingerly got to her feet somewhat like a camel, one end at a time. After several exploratory pokes, she evidently decided she could navigate under her own power and came over beside me at the window. The sunlight made her hair shine. I was going to miss that, too. She took my arm and very gently led me to the couch and pushed me down on it. She stood in front of me with arms folded and just looked at me. I resented being treated like an idiot.

"Now you listen to me for a minute," she began. "You've been having one hell of a fine time working yourself up to a good second-act curtain and it's all a lot of nonsense."

"That's all right for you to say. You're not wanted for murder." I started to get up and she pushed me back down again. I considered swatting her.

"But that's the point," she went on. "You didn't kill that old battle-axe, did you? Or did you?"

"Of course not, but…"

"Then as far as I can see all you did was not tell somebody you found her murdered—if she was murdered, which I doubt. It might have been an accident."

"I took the book away."

"That's another thing. Why ever did you do that?"

"Well, it had my name on it and your name on it and that would have meant that we were there, and there you are."

"So what? I wasn't there." Then her eyes got very round and she suddenly bent over as if to kiss me, but midway she yelped from the reminders that she wasn't quite capable of such action yet. "But you, darling, you were trying to shield me. I think you're wonderful. Let's have another drink." And we did and I began to feel better. It's nice being thought a gentleman capable of shielding someone from something. We got all the pillows from the chairs and couch and put them on the floor and lay down with our drinks.

"Now then," I said, after we were comfortable. "What were you about to be all stern about a minute ago?"

"It's all really too simple. You've done all the wrong things so far just because you're a ham at heart and you felt you had to pad your part. Anybody but an actor would have given a yell and, when people started to come running, said 'look what I found' but not you, you little Hamlet you… Oh, no… Well, anyway you've done it and that's that. As it stands now we've got two choices. You can call up the police right now and tell them all about it. How you are going to alibi taking that filthy book I have no idea."

"What's the other choice?" I asked. "If I do that it will mean a lot of explaining. I'm liable for attempting to obstruct justice or concealing evidence, or something."

"Then we could just assume that you did put your gloves back on or someone messed up your prints after you left, and then we could burn the Youth and Beauty Book to a crisp and cast the ashes off the Triboro Bridge."

That sounded good so far.

"And then what?"

"Then we'll just say no more about it."

"Oh, fine. But don't forget the book was open on her desk and the heavy of the piece might have seen our names as well as one Bobby LeB., whoever the hell *he* is."

"Then I think a bit of dialogue with Mr. LeB. is clearly indicated. Very subtle-like…underplayed, but very, very fraught. Where does he live?"

"I don't even know *who* he is much less where he lives."

"Then maybe it's all in the Youth and Beauty Book. Practically everything else is, God knows. Get it up!"

I got it up. The dried blood didn't make the job any more appetizing. Nellie had not been the most efficient person in the world, and the book had, on the whole, somewhat the aspect of a sheaf of used Kleenex.

Slips of paper with phone numbers and random addresses were stuck all through, as well as some empty envelopes and dull-looking bills, even her bank book.

After a couple of hours we had to give up the search for Bobby LeB.'s address. Though, as Maggie pointed out, we certainly discovered a lot of unmarried actors and actresses whom we never suspected before, answering to the same phone numbers. The only information we could discover about Mr. LeB. was that the last year he had several appointments with Nellie, but not at any regular intervals and he was always entered only as Bobby LeB. or once or twice simply B. B., which we took to mean our boy.

I got interested in her bank book. Nellie was doing a great deal better financially than either of us would have imagined. You would have gathered from her books that what money she did have she made selling shoestrings and gum, along with Apple Annie, in theater lobbies. But according to her bank book she was almost in the surtax brackets. Every month for the last year there was a five-hundred-dollar lump deposit in addition to littler ones during the month. My nose began to twitch as I pointed this out to Maggie.

"Obviously blackmail."

She was not impressed.

"Oh, really! It was a sad day for the world when you discovered circulating libraries."

"But how else can you explain it? You know she didn't cast that many shows."

"Maybe she had an income. Maybe she had property. People do get five hundred dollars a month without resorting to blackmail."

"But that would explain everything. Why she was murdered."

"Here we go again. Timmy, look me in the eye." I did. "Do you really believe all that junk?"

"No, I guess not. Not really."

"Then that's all right. Otherwise I might start worrying." I stuffed the bank book back in the Youth and Beauty Book and tossed it on the floor.

"Well, what do we do now?"

"I know a man who used to be in naval intelligence during the war. I'll bet he could help us. We could certainly use a little intelligence around here. Do you want me to call him up?"

"Let me try first before we send for the fleet," I said.

"Well, I only wanted to be helpful. Have you eaten?"

"No. Have you?"

"I'm starved. Let's go to Sardi's for lunch."

"Oh, no we won't," I said.

"The murderer always returns to the scene of his crime."

"My pal!"

"Well, why not? You've done all the wrong things so far. One more couldn't make much difference. We can drop in at Nellie's office casual-like and you can get a quick swipe at that doorknob, and we can pitch that damned book in a corner of her office and just forget all about it."

I helped her up off the floor.

"Okay. What can we lose?"

She went into the bedroom to dress while I had

another drink, but it didn't help much. I started to get depressed all over again. I took my drink and leaned against the bedroom door.

"You know, Maggie, if you cut down on your drinking and got more sleep you'd be a good-looking girl. Somebody might even marry you again."

"Why, thank you, darling. But who? And why the overwhelming flattery? What have I done to deserve it?" She stopped brushing her hair and looked at me in the mirror. For some reason I felt a little embarrassed.

"It just seems kind of pointless all this nipping about, frittering around in the theater. Where does it get you?" She swiveled around from her dressing table.

"What about you?"

"Never mind me. Besides, I can't do anything else. The theater's all I know."

"You did all right in the army. People told me. I asked."

"Oh, the army. That's different. Latch on to a good sergeant and you can't miss."

"It's none of my business, I know," Maggie said earnestly. "But do you mean to just keep on like this…you know what I mean…sort of…I mean, not ever…well, you know what I mean…" She finished lamely, strangely shy for her.

Yes, of course, I knew what she meant. And no, of course I didn't mean to keep on like this. I was a man with a plan. A three-year plan. Operation Hollywood. I wanted to be an actor! So I made a bargain with myself while waiting in a cigarette camp near Le Havre to be shipped home. Three years to get a good part on Broadway or back to the salt mines.

It all seemed so simple—in Le Havre.

Who gets all the best parts in New York? Movie actors. Okay, so get to be a movie actor. How? Well, first you've got to be seen in the right places, get a little publicity. That's the magic—publicity. And in the right places you'll meet the right people who'll maybe give you a small part and then maybe your picture in the paper and bingo!—a screen test and a contract. Six months on the coast and six months in New York for a play. Then every day is Christmas and you even plan whose stocking will be hanging up beside yours.

That was thirty-five months ago and gives you a rough idea how punchy you can get after four years in the army.

Four weeks more and Operation Hollywood would end with a whimper and with it my chance for the big money. But a bargain's a bargain. I hope I hadn't forgotten how to pilot a bulldozer.

There was no point in telling all this to Maggie—now. If things had only worked out differently...

"Timmy, what *is* the matter with you?"

"What? Oh, nothing. Just indulging in a little wishful thinking."

"What about?"

"Hoping I'm not going to spend the rest of my all-too-brief life running away from a murder rap."

"Oh." Maggie turned back to the mirror and finished

her face. I went over to the closet and got out her mink coat and helped her on with it. I wrapped my arms around her and stood that way for a moment. I needed someone to hang on to. I buried my face in the shoulder of her coat. It was cool and faintly perfumed. She reached up and patted my cheek.

"Now stop worrying. Everything's going to be all right."

While I was out in the hall putting on my coat she brought the Youth and Beauty Book.

"Here." She handed it to me. "You ought to be able to drop it in a corner easily while you're messing up your fingerprints."

"I expect so." I stuck it in my breast pocket. "But you know as well as I do that fingerprints or no, eventually they're going to find out I was in Nellie's office this morning."

"Nonsense."

"It isn't nonsense. They always do."

"How?"

"I don't know, but they always do. One leaves spoors or something."

"Does one? How awful."

"And unless they find out who did it, I can't prove I didn't, when it comes right down to it."

"Then by all means we must find out who did do it."

It seemed so simple the way she said it.

## CHAPTER FOUR

I LOOKED AT MY WATCH as we pulled up in front of
Sardi's. Only four hours since I had been here before
and it seemed like four years.

The meter said eighty cents and Maggie gave me a
dollar, which I gave to the driver, and we got out.

The sidewalk in front of Sardi's is strictly Actors'
Equity property. From ten in the morning till one at night
you can always find one standing there. Musicians have
their own Wailing Wall around Fiftieth Street somewhere;
vaudevillians in front of the Palace; the radio people, a
sheltered lot, have theirs on the third floor of NBC or CBS
on Madison. Models are around Grand Central and Park,
but actors are loyal to Forty-fourth Street between Eighth
and Broadway. And they were there in full force today,
and it didn't take long for Maggie and me to find out that
Nellie had been discovered.

Just about my most unfavorite actor in the world
would have to have the pleasure of telling us what we
already knew only too well. He spied us standing by the
curb and came rushing over. Ted Kent is his name, or at
least that is what he uses. I suppose the basic reason I

don't like him is very simple; he always gets all the parts I want and when you get right down to it, that's the main reason most actors don't like other actors they don't like.

Ted is about my height, maybe a couple of inches shorter without his trick you-can-be-taller-than-she-is shoes and is a perfect example of a successful Operation Hollywood. The right people, the publicity, the small part, the screen test and the Hollywood contract. Only they didn't pick up his option so he headed straight back to Broadway with quite a bit of money and new teeth, trying to get that part that will shoot him back to the coast again.

As he greeted us, he gave me a very small hello, which was all right by me, and Maggie a very big kiss— which wasn't.

"Maggie, *darling*. Have you heard?" He was a *darling* boy, too. "Nellie is *dead!*" And he sort of stood back on one foot and waited for us to take it big. We must have both felt it was better to play dumb and we did what was obviously expected.

"No!" said Maggie. "Who did it?"

Ted gave her what I thought was a funny look and said, "But, darling, nobody *did* it. She just collapsed. Heart, I expect."

"Are you sure?" I said.

"What do you mean, am I sure? Of course I'm sure. Heart failure, I think, or drunk—you know she drank like a fish. Anyway, she fell over on that spindle she had on her desk, you know." I admitted I did know. "And she died. File and forget, I say." He practically giggled at that one. Maggie and I looked at each other. I think my sigh of relief must have reached the East River.

"How do you know?" Maybe he wasn't straight on his facts. Maybe this was all just a trick by the police to find out who really did it. When you've convinced yourself that you are a key witness in a murder scene it's a little disconcerting to be told that it isn't a murder at all and just a simple case of alcohol or heart failure. I can't say I was sorry that it was turning out this way, but I'm afraid the ham in me was feeling cheated as if I had been fired from a show before it even started rehearsals.

Ted tried to wither me with a look, but I don't wither very easy by guys like Ted. "Everybody knows. The police have been here asking questions and having a big time. They're still up in her office now waiting for the meat wagon." You could tell in his day he'd been in some pretty lousy shows, too. A couple of other people joined our clump attracted by Ted's overloud voice—which was the idea—and, goosed up by a bigger audience, Ted really put out.

"Libby Drew found her…she was just dropping in, making the rounds, and saw her lying on her desk, blood all over the place running over the floor…"

"But…" I started to interrupt but Maggie silenced me with a stiff poke in the ribs. Ted chose to ignore my attempted interruption and went merrily on, practically drooling at the mouth.

"Of course, you know Libby, sly puss that she is…. Did she make with the screams and bring everybody running as anyone else would do it?" He answered himself. "No indeed, the little brat carefully took the elevator down to the main floor, probably pulled her dress off one shoulder, put eyeshadow under her eyes and staggered all the way across the street into Sardi's and announced it like a messenger in *Macbeth*. What a performance! Nothing like it since the Cherry sisters. I was having lunch with Terry and Lawrence.... They're doing a new show and there's the dream part for me..."

"Okay, okay," I said. "Cut to the finish." He gave me a nasty look but went on with his story....

"Well, you can imagine what a stir there was. The place was jammed to the ears. Vincent Sardi called the police right away, and everyone tore out and up to her office. And sure enough there she was dead as a door nail. What a crush in that little office. Everyone was there. Stanley and Brock and Cheryl and George..."

"Spare us the society notes. Then what?" I said.

"Well, after a while the police came and all of us except Libby had to leave."

A policeman wandered about muttering for the crowd to break it up and move along, but after a while gave it up as a bad job because you can't break up a crowd of actors. They just shift into other groupings. Ted took off his hat, held it in his teeth and pulled out a pocket comb and combed his hair. Maggie and I just stood there watching him. When every hair and wave was arranged to his satisfaction he wiped off the comb, stuck it back in his pocket, carefully replaced his hat and kissed Maggie on the cheek again.

"Well, darling, I've got to fly. Let's have lunch one

day. I'll call you. Be sure and see the morning papers, I think my picture's in them. Of course Libby hogged most of them. But the lad from the *Brooklyn Eagle* was very nice. Remembered me from my last picture with Paramount. Bye now." And he was off down the street headed toward Broadway.

"Let's have a drink before I vomit." I took Maggie's arm and led her into Sardi's.

## CHAPTER FIVE

SARDI'S RESTAURANT IS REALLY just one big room divided by some chest-high partitions with benches or, in the chi-chier places, I expect they would be called banquettes. All the woodwork is dark brown and the chairs and benches are covered with dark leather and the walls are shingled with caricatures of well-known theatrical people. Needless to say, one of me is not included. New ones are added from time to time, I suppose, though I don't know where they find the room to hang them, unless it's the ladies' room.

It was almost empty when Maggie and I came in. Just a few people were scattered around starting the five o'clock jump a little early. Just like we had been doing all day. We sat down and ordered drinks. Maggie shed her mink and pulled off her hat. I lit her a cigarette. She took a deep drag, blew it out and slumped back against the wall. I was slumping some, too; I was feeling definitely let down and very, very tired.

"Anyway it was fun while it lasted." Maggie smiled at me. "You know I feel kind of sorry for the old gal. Heart failure. I didn't know she had a weak heart. I didn't even suspect she had a heart for that matter."

"I don't think it was heart failure."

"Oh, Timmy, now don't start that murder game again. You'd think someone had broken your bicycle or something. So you're not a wanted man…you're still young…there's still something to live for…if you're real good and eat your broccoli you may find another body one day."

"All the same, did you ever step on a nail when you were a kid?"

"No, I've never enjoyed that sort of thing."

"Well, I have lots of times, and with my full weight on it it didn't go in even an inch."

"You can scarcely compare the bottom of your foot with Nellie's right mammary gland, after all."

"There's not that much difference."

"Well, dear, you ought to know."

"Oh, shut up." Then I remembered what Ted Kent had said. "Still, one way to find out—I might ask Libby Drew what the police thought when they found Nellie."

"Knowing Libby, if it would help get her picture in the paper, I'm surprised she didn't confess to doing in Nellie herself."

I nudged Maggie as the front door swung open and Henry Frobisher walked in. We watched him as he slowly came across the room and sat down at a wall table, two away from us. I'd been wondering about him, off and on, all afternoon. Frobisher had billing in the Youth and Beauty Book, too. An appointment with Nellie at three-thirty this afternoon. It was now about four-thirty and had Nellie been alive, he would have been just coming from it.

I'd put Frobisher at around fifty-five and, although it had started creeping back, he was by no means a scratch-bait boy yet. Maybe it was the sunlamp tan, or, maybe, his eyebrows bleached out more than his brown hair, which was graying at the proper places; anyway, his eyebrows blended strangely into his high forehead and made his face look naked.

His newest show, *A Kiss Thrown In,* starring Louise Randall, had been in rehearsal for two weeks and I couldn't tell whether it was going badly, or whether Nellie's death had upset him. No matter what caused it, I have never seen a man look so tired and still move. He sat back, ordered a drink and looked around the room. His gaze finally hit us and he gave us a vague smile. But I wasn't going to waste any chances to talk to any producers, even if he didn't have anything for me in his show....

"Wasn't that awful about Nellie?" I said across two tables.

"Yes, tragic, tragic." He seemed to be looking right through me.

"I didn't know she had a weak heart, did you?"

"No. No, I didn't." He looked at Maggie. "Good afternoon, Mrs. Lanson."

"Good afternoon, Mr. Frobisher. How's the show going?"

"Still pretty rough. We're doing a bit of rewriting." Maggie didn't need a job and I did. I wanted to be in on the conversation.

"Mr. Frobisher, you knew Nellie pretty well, didn't you? I mean, she cast most of your shows and all that."

"Yes, I've known Nellie for a good many years, fine woman."

"Well then." I leaned toward him. "Can you think of any enemies she might have had?"

"Enemies?" He looked a little startled at that, and I noticed for the first time that his eyes were almost green. "Good heavens no, what makes you ask that?"

"Don't mind him, Mr. Frobisher." Maggie pulled me gently back against the wall. "He's been in so many mysteries, he's trying to make one out of this."

Mr. Frobisher picked up his drink and came over and sat down on the bench next to me.

"I don't understand what you mean. Do you think she was killed? Murdered?"

I had been thinking that to myself ever since I had found her, but now that someone else said it it sounded a little foolish. Something in Frobisher's manner of asking it, his soft, rather clipped voice, seemed to make my even having thought it vulgar and very corny.

"No, I guess not," I finally admitted. "But did you ever step on a nail when you were a kid?"

The moment I said it I felt ridiculous.

"No, I don't believe I ever did. I may have, though it's been a long time since I was a kid." *Wistful* is the word, I think, for the smile that followed. "But what has my not having stepped on a nail got to do with Nellie?"

"Well, you know that thing she fell on, the desk spindle…it wasn't much larger than a good-size nail."

"You seem to know a good deal about it." I could feel

my face starting to redden, so I took a quick gulp of my old-fashioned.

"Oh, I've been going to see Nellie for about ten years, and that office hasn't changed a speck of dust in all that time."

"But I still don't see why you think she was murdered."

Maggie was getting bored and she started shrugging on her coat. Frobisher and I helped her.

"It's pure frustration, Mr. Frobisher. Nellie called him in about a job this morning, and he thinks it's very inconsiderate of her to die before he got it. Which reminds me. We ought to send flowers. Do you know where the funeral's going to be?"

"Why yes, I find myself rather in charge. Tomorrow, three o'clock, the Henderson Funeral Home." He turned to me. "I'd appreciate it if you would be a pallbearer and help get the casket to the station. Her niece is coming up from Hopkinsville, Kentucky, to take the body back there for burial."

I said I'd be glad to. As a matter of fact, I was very flattered that he had asked me.

"If you were a friend of hers, Mrs. Lanson, perhaps you'd like to come, too?"

"Thank you," said Maggie. "I would, very much." She stood up. "Well, goodbye, Mr. Frobisher, and good luck on your show."

I left money for the drinks and a tip on the table, making a mental note to nail Maggie for her share. Mr. Frobisher stood up with us.

"Goodbye, Mrs. Lanson, and thank you." He looked

at me. "Goodbye." I got my hat and coat from Renee and it wasn't till we got out on Forty-fourth Street that I realized that in spite of my blue-shirt lead performance, Mr. Frobisher didn't even know my name.

# CHAPTER SIX

MAGGIE REALLY NEEDN'T have been in such a hurry to leave even if her plaster was itching. After all, it wasn't every day I got the chance to have a drink with a producer and she shouldn't have blatted out that I had an appointment with Nellie that morning and I told her so.

"I'm dreadfully sorry, angel, but you were rather tiresome about it. All that nail rigmarole. Besides, my bottom hurts like blazes."

We started walking toward Broadway, and I began to feel ashamed of myself. Actually, what difference did it make to me? I had missed out on a job. That's happened before. But, nevertheless, I couldn't help feeling there was something fishy about it. It must have been all because of that damned Bobby LeB. I tried to explain this to Maggie.

"Then for heaven's sake find him and get it out of your system. You won't be happy till you do. It oughtn't to be too difficult. Equity could tell you how many LeB.'s there are—if he's an actor, and I can't imagine anyone willingly setting foot in Nellie's rats' nest unless he were. Incidentally, with all your starry-eye-making at Frobisher, we forgot to eat. Let's go into Walgreen's."

As we tried to weave through the mob of bobby-sox autograph hunters waiting for the Paramount performers to come out of the stage door, one of the more unappetizing ones disengaged herself from the rest of the covey, sauntered over, and stood right in front of me shoving a grimy autograph book and pen in my face. She wore the usual year-round uniform: saddle shoes, plaid skirt and sweater.

"Sign here, will you?" she commanded. "And make it 'To Bertha Oliphant with love.'"

"Why do you want my autograph?" I asked. "I'm not famous."

"You're an actor, aren't you?"

"Yes."

"Well, Rome wasn't built in a day. Sign here." Pleased, I signed with protestations of undying love to Bertha Oliphant.

"Jeez, thanks," she said when she read my love note. "That's swell." She started to go back.

"Don't you want mine, too?" asked Maggie.

"What for?" asked Bertha.

"I'm an actress," said Maggie.

"Don't give me that stuff, lady. And paper costs money."

"What makes you think I'm not an actress?"

"Listen, lady," said Bertha patiently, "it's the mink. If you're an actress and got a mink coat, I know you. And I don't know you." This put Maggie in her place.

"But why did you want my autograph?" I asked. "You don't know me."

"Well, I'll tell you, I'm different, see. I'm what you

might call a speculator. Them other jerks over there—"
she tossed her head in the direction of the other autograph hounds "—they just get people already famous."
She sniffed contemptuously. "I think you gotta look
ahead. How do I know, someday you might amount to
something."

"Do you stop everybody that comes along this
street?" I asked her. I was starting to get an idea.

"Of course not. Only people who look like they're
gonna be something."

"Thank you, I'm sure," said Maggie.

"You're doin' all right, kid," said Bertha, eyeing the
mink.

"Were you here this morning?" I asked her.

"Sure I was."

"Could you let me see the ones you collected this
morning?"

"What for?" Bertha asked suspiciously. "You want
to buy some? If you're in the market I got some exclu-
sives, home."

"I want to see if somebody passed by about eleven
o'clock."

"What's the name? Lots of people passed here."

"Bobby LeB.," I said, "I don't know his last name,
just LeB."

"Why, Timmy, aren't you clever," said Maggie.

"It's just a chance." But Bertha squelched it.

"Nope. No Bobby LeB.'s this morning. Never
heard of him."

"Can I see your book anyway?"

"I tell you I ain't got no Bobby LeB., or whatever the hell his name is, so you're just wasting my time." It took a dollar to persuade her. "Okay. This part here's the ones I got this morning."

There were only about seven, and I was disgusted to see that just before mine was Ted Kent's. The third sheet down, however, was blank with an inky smear across it as though a pen had been dug into it. I asked Bertha what that was for.

"Oh, that lousy rat. Damn near ruined my fountain pen. New one, too."

"What did he do?"

"Oh, he got snotty when I asked him to sign. Wish I'd belted him." She looked like she was just the girl that could do it.

"Do you remember what he looked like?" I practically had on my two-visored cap and a meerschaum.

"Sure I do. Never forget him. Had on them dark glasses, kinda peaky. You know."

"Harlequin... Yes, go on."

"Yeah, well he had on a pair of them harlequin gimmicks and a polo coat, and he was carrying a box. A big one. He jabbed me with it while I was holding up my book and new pen. Ruined the whole sheet."

"Why did you ask him to sign in the first place? Did he look important?"

"Well, not important, maybe. Different sort of."

"How different?"

"Jeez, I don't know. Just different. You have to know about things like that. I can't tell you exactly. Oh—

oh…here comes Charlie." She snatched back the book and was off in hot pursuit. We started again for Walgreen's. Perhaps I was getting somewhere. The time was right.…

"Honestly, Tim." Maggie looked at me admiringly. "You amaze me."

"I amaze myself, sometimes," I said modestly for what I considered a tasty bit of sleuthing. A murderer *would* be nasty about signing his name.

"But it's so silly. In the first place this Bobby may not look like an actor at all."

"He'd have to with that name."

"It's perfectly asinine to expect that rude little girl would ask him for his autograph."

"Just because she didn't want yours is no reason…"

"What's more, there are at least three other ways he could have gone—west toward Eighth Avenue, through Shubert Alley and on the other side of this street. For that matter he might have taken a taxi." I wasn't feeling quite so pleased with myself now.

"Maggie, do you honestly believe it is all as simple as they say? Heart failure?"

"I don't believe anything about it, one way or the other. It's none of my affair nor, actually, is it yours, now. I always thought playing Private Eye would be sheer heaven. But you know how silly the whole idea is. You're just getting out of character, darling. Stick to your top hat and cigarettes and don't try making with the derby and cigars. Go ahead, try and find your Bobby LeB., if it's going to keep you awake nights. That's perfectly harmless, but leave that other stuff to the boys who can't dance divinely, or you'll get in trouble."

And she was so right!

## CHAPTER SEVEN

IN WALGREEN'S THERE WAS just the usual crowd of civilians. It was way past even the most leisurely lunchtime for actors. No matter how good you were at it, you couldn't nurse an egg-salad sandwich and chocolate malted till almost four-thirty.

I ordered a ham and cheese and coffee, and Maggie had a tuna-fish salad and coffee. We just sat there until the plates came sliding up. I always meant to find out how they manage to get two slices out of one leaf of lettuce. It wasn't till I started eating that I realized how hungry I was so I ordered another of the same. After we finished I reached for a cigarette and felt the tickets that Nick Stein had given me.

"Would you like to go to the theater tonight?" I asked Maggie.

"Is it a real show or some more of your passes?" She'd been with me before and was naturally a little suspicious.

"That new Lucille Blake thing. Not supposed to be too bad."

"Oh, I don't think so. Not tonight. I still feel a little strange and you must admit that this has been a rather hectic day. First that damn doorknob and then you rushing in and confessing to a murder. Why don't you ask your precious Bobby LeB. to go?"

"Not a bad idea if I knew where to find him. Might take Libby Drew and find out what she knows."

"She'd be thrilled to death. Which reminds me I didn't pay for the drinks."

She reached into her purse and put some money in my hand. I didn't see how much it was. "Here, take this and pay for them, will you? You can pay me back from the reward."

"What reward?"

"Why else are you so intent on playing Dick Tracy?"

"I still owe you some." But I didn't try to give it back.

"Yes, dear, I know, but don't let it keep you awake nights. It doesn't me. Call me in the morning and let me know what Libby does for you…in solving your precious little mystery, I mean." She patted my cheek. "But don't forget Nellie's funeral in the afternoon. She'll give a better show dead than Lucille Blake alive."

And knowing an exit line when she says one, Maggie walked out of the drugstore pulling on her gloves. A nice girl. Has sense, too, though you generally overlook it when she starts being vague; but this afternoon she wasn't vague at all. I knew she was right. It was silly, I suppose, getting myself mixed up in this Nellie thing. Maybe I was just bored. I felt bored a lot since I got out of the army, but who didn't. Hell, I might as well finish it up now that I had started. Call up Libby and see if she wanted to go to the theater tonight. I gathered the checks and walked over to the cashiers. It was then that I looked at the money Maggie had put in my hand. Two fifty-dollar bills...enough to last me for a month, if I was very careful. The cashier gave me some nickels with the change, so I went down to the deserted basement and telephoned Libby. She was delighted to go to the theater with me and would meet me at Louis Bergen's bar at eight-fifteen, and I'd better get the *Bronx Home News* or some such paper tomorrow, she might have her picture in it. I told her I would and hung up.

The clock on the wall said it was only about ten minutes to five...a lot sure had happened in one day. That's what comes of getting up before noon.

If I hurried I might have time to get over to Equity before it closed. Then I could ride home on the Fifth Avenue bus and maybe catch a nap before meeting Libby.

The old brownstone on West Forty-seventh Street where Equity has its offices is something right out of Charles Addams and the only reason I ever go there is to advise them of a change in my address or see if the bond is posted for that turkey I may get a walk-on in.

I climbed the creaky stairs up to the third floor information section where they have all the addresses. The fussy little old lady in charge behind the wire fence was just getting ready to go. She was alone—her handmaidens must have jumped the gun. With a great deal of pursing of lips, she finally consented to ask me what I wanted.

"Yiss? And what is it you require?"

"It's kind of silly," I said. "But I'm trying to locate

someone, but I only know his first name and last initial."
I gave her the teeth, but she was having none of it.

"Are you an Equity member?"

"Yes, for eight years. My name is Tim Briscoe." This
seemed to mean something to her.

"Briscoe...Briscoe? Oh, yes. Someone just asked for
your address and phone number not half an hour ago."

"Who was it? Do you remember?"

"Certainly. It was dear Henry Frobisher. Such a fine
man, a real gentleman. I was with him in *Bless You,
Darling.* Perhaps you saw it?" I hadn't. She preened
herself and patted her hair back in place. "Of course, it
was just a tiny part, the party scene in the second act. I
wore purple and ecru lace. Dear Henry was so kind
about the part being so small, but I do think it better to
have a small part with a first-rate management than a
lead with some fly-by-night, don't you?" I heartily
agreed. She rambled on.

Why would Frobisher want to see me? And I thought
he didn't even know my name. I wondered if it was too
late to call him. No, he didn't look like he was going
back to his office when we left him. Anyway, Kendall
Thayer was at the Casbah and he was pretty good about
taking messages for me.

"And wasn't that tragic about his son?" Purple and
Ecru Lace was still rolling along.

"His son?" I wasn't paying much attention, trying to
puzzle out why he should want my phone number.

"Being killed in the war. Such a blow to dear Mr.
Frobisher. An only son, too. I met him once, you know."

"No, I didn't know." And I didn't want to know. I just wanted to get Bobby's address and beat it home and find out if Frobisher had called and if so why. But Tootsie, here, was determined to take me down Memory Lane, willy-nilly. "Such a lovely boy, too. So well mannered. Mr. Frobisher brought him to rehearsal. Such a tragedy. Were you in the service, too?" I admitted I was. "Mr. Frobisher's son was killed in action. In Normandy, I believe," she said accusingly. Well, my God, Tootsie, I'm sorry. I apologize. I did not mean to offend you. I know I'm not lovely or very well mannered, and my father can't give you a job in purple and ecru lace, but please don't make me feel guilty just being alive.

"I'm sorry, Mrs....Mrs...."

"Tuckerman. Mrs. Tuckerman. Of course, my stage name was Marianne Rice, but then..."

"Yes, well, Mrs. Tuckerman, I'm really in rather a hurry...."

"Oh, yiss, of course," she said coldly, all efficiency again. "Now who was it you wanted to locate? It's really past hours, you know." I told her what I knew and she flew to the files.

"We have a Robert LeBor, but he is in Hollywood now. Would he be the one?"

"No, I shouldn't think so. Any others?"

"There's a Robin LeBaron...but of course he's dead, poor soul, so I should scarcely think he would be the one you are after, would you?"

"Scarcely. Is that all?"

"Yiss, that is all. Are you quite sure he is a member of Actors' Equity?"

"No…not exactly."

"Well, really, Mr. Briscoe." Angrily she took her coat from a cupboard and started to put it on.

"Can you suggest any other place I might look? You've been so kind and helpful perhaps you might know some other place." That thawed her out a little. She paused for a second.

"Is your friend a member of the profession?"

"I'm almost positive of that."

"There are still, you know, other organizations. Professional organizations—AFRA, Screen Actors Guild, Chorus Equity and, I believe, those night club entertainers have some sort of an organization, too." I hadn't thought of that possibility. My thanks were slightly overdone, but she must receive a kind word so seldom that by the time I had escorted her down to the street and said goodbye I was pretty sure I could play gin rummy with those address cards from now on.

There must be someone I knew who was a member of those other unions, and I could get them to check for me. It was such a long shot that there didn't seem to be any particular need for secrecy. And if questioned, I could always say I found a watch or a ring with an inscription. "Ever thine, Bobby LeB.," or some such.

And Mr. Frobisher wanted my phone number. Money in my pocket and a phone call from a top-flight producer. What more could I ask?

Things were certainly looking up.

## CHAPTER EIGHT

I GOT OFF THE BUS AT Washington Square and walked to the Casbah. Kendall Thayer was sitting in my room when I opened the door, calmly reading all my old letters.... I don't particularly like people reading my mail and told him so.

"My dear boy, these are as nothing." He wasn't the slightest bit ruffled at being caught in the act. "If you like I'll show you some of my fan mail...show you what real passion is." He tossed mine back in the bureau drawer. "These are all just amateurs...no finesse, no imagination."

"It's just too damn bad about that, and get the hell out of here and stay out, and if I ever catch you in here again I'll knock your ears off." I was getting very angry.

"Calm yourself, my boy. Wounded vanity that is all. Besides, you had phone calls."

"Well, why didn't you say so?" I took off my coat and hat and threw them on the bed. Kendall immediately snatched up my hat and handed it back to me. "Say, what's the idea?" I had a good mind to punch him, old as he was.

"Don't you know that it is bad luck to put a hat on a bed?"

"Never mind that." But I took the hat and threw it on the shelf in the closet. "What about those calls?" He handed me a slip of paper.

"That's how I happened to come across your letters, looking for a piece of paper." I didn't say anything, but looked at the slip. Mr. Frobisher and Mrs. Lanson, both, wanted me to call them as soon as I got in. And Diana, the woman I had been out with last night, had called...no message.

"I trust that means you have a job with Mr. Frobisher."

Kendall helped himself to the pack of cigarettes when I was getting one for myself. I didn't feel so annoyed with him now so I let him get away with it.

"But his show's already in rehearsal."

"There's many a slip before opening night. Fine man, Mr. Frobisher. I remember when I was with him in *Star Light*.... I was just back from the coast.... I had a scene...." I quickly shut off this scrapbook browsing. I'd heard it all before. Kendall had a memory like a library, and with that memory...

"Kendall, did you ever hear of anyone named Bobby LeB.?"

"Bobby Le Bee? What a curious name... No, I'm sure I should remember it if I had."

"LeB. is just the initials of his last name—L, E, capital B."

"There was a Robert LeBor who's a director in pictures now. Just an assistant director when I knew him. Is he the one you mean?"

"No, he's in Hollywood. Any others?"

"Well, a Robin LeBaron died several years ago. I never knew him personally, though I think he was considered quite good. Of course I was on the coast at the time." I could have saved myself a trip to Equity if I'd thought of Kendall first.

"No, I know about those two. Any others…" He seemed to be poking about in that rye-soaked brain for another one but he couldn't quite make it.

"It seems to me there was another one somewhere along the line…. I'm not very good on names." He was doing all right. "But I never forget a face. I can't quite seem to place him. It's a rather unusual name. Now let me see…"

"Well, don't strain yourself. Beat it now, I want to make some calls. But if you remember, let me know. By the way, I suppose you heard that Nellie Brant is dead?" His reaction was a momentary expression of definite pleasure before he could pull that old saggy face into the proper grimace of sadness. Why is it old people are glad when other people die? Or is it just actors?

"Why, no…I didn't know. I haven't been out of the house all day." He evidently forgot the trip to the liquor store for whiskey with the two bucks I had given him this morning.

"Was she dead when you got there?" That startled me.

"When I got where?"

"Why, I thought you told me you had an appointment with her this morning." I didn't remember telling him anything of the kind, but I may have. This morning I wasn't playing it so cozy. Still it did give me a start.

"Did I? Well, I was wrong. It was somebody else."

"Sure. I probably just misunderstood you."

"Yes, I guess you did."

"We played together, you know. She was with me on *Front Page Stuff*."

"No, I didn't know." It had never even occurred to me she'd been an actress. "What was she like?"

"A brilliant comedienne. I remember we had one scene together. I was playing Lord Washburn…pearl-gray cutaway. She mistook me for the butler—very amusing. That scene took all the notices. I think I still have them if you would care to look at them. Mr. Frobisher was stage manager then, you know." I hadn't known that, either. But, like agents, producers don't spring full-fledged out of sea foam.

"What happened to Nellie? Why did she stop acting if she was so hot?"

"Another great tragedy of the theater." Presumably he meant he was the first. "She was a singer, and, I believe, she strained her vocal cords or something, because after a while she couldn't sing anymore."

"Okay, scram, will you, Kendall? I told you I've got to phone." I started looking up Frobisher's number in the phone book. Kendall strode majestically to the door, which, in my cheese-box, takes some doing. He rested one hand on the door casing and gave me burning stare No. 6A with all the stops out.

"I go." Pause. "I go to return anon."

"Yeah, yeah, okay." I began dialing Frobisher's number. Kendall relaxed.

"You wouldn't, perchance, have a couple more fish swimming around loose, would you?"

"No, I wouldn't." I made a mistake in the number and had to start over again. "Get the hell out, will you?" I threw the telephone book at him, but he closed the door too soon and it just hit the door and slapped to the floor.

A clipped British accent finally allowed me to speak to Mr. Frobisher.

"Mr. Frobisher, this is Tim Briscoe. You asked me to call you?"

"Oh, yes, Tim. I wondered if you would be available for a part in a show I have in rehearsal?" How available can you get?

"I believe so, Mr. Frobisher. Of course, I have a couple of things on the fire...."

"It's a small part in the last act. I've had someone rehearsing it for two weeks, but I'm afraid he isn't working out. Frankly, you just stand around and look attractive until it's time to wind up the plot, but you'll have a few good lines and they take doing. The part pays a hundred and a quarter. Would you be interested?"

"What do I wear?" If I was going to have to buy a new suit, maybe I could get more money.

"Just a dinner jacket. You can supply that, can't you?"

"Yes, sir." I certainly had a dinner jacket.

"I know this is rushing things a bit, but we open in less than a fortnight. How about it?"

"I'd be glad to, Mr. Frobisher." There didn't seem to be much point arguing about money. He could get hundreds of actors who would jump at the chance to be in a Frobisher show for minimum.

"Fine. It's settled, then. Eleven tomorrow morning at the Lyceum Theater and I've made an appointment for you at Hans Trindler's studio for publicity photographs at nine, if that's convenient." Convenient? Trindler was only the best photographer in the business.

"That's perfectly convenient, sir."

"Good. I'll see you at the Lyceum tomorrow at eleven." He started to hang up.

"Oh, Mr. Frobisher. There's just one thing, if you don't mind my asking. How did you happen to pick me?"

"Today at Sardi's. You see, it does pay to drink a little." So I hadn't been fooling him.

"And I thought you didn't even know my name."

He chuckled. "As a matter of fact I didn't, I asked Renee." God bless Renee the hat-check girl. I'd have to give her a bigger tip from now on. "I'll see that you get your contract in the next few days. Goodbye."

That's the way it goes. You beat your brains out banging on agents' and producers' doors and what do you get? Nothing. But you happen to have a drink in a bar at a certain time and you end up with a job at a hundred and a quarter per—or that's what I told myself. As I furiously dialed Maggie's number to tell her the good news, I really believed I had been offered that part because Mr. Frobisher thought I would look attractive standing around until it was time to wind up the plot. Well, part of that was true.

Maggie finally answered.

"This is Tim. Guess what."

"You, too?"

"Frobisher, you mean?"

"Lyceum Theater, eleven tomorrow. You, too?"

"Yes, isn't it marvelous?" I said.

"I just can't believe it."

"And Trindler is taking my picture tomorrow morning for the show."

"He's already got some of me on file, but promise me you'll give me one of you."

"I promise."

"Frobisher said I was only a small part in the last act."

"Me, too. I wear a dinner jacket and look attractive."

"A cinch. I'm having a fitting at Chez Ernest tomorrow at ten for my dress. Jenny Pittenger is doing the sets and supervising the clothes. I hope I get something good."

"Chez Ernest?" I said. "But that was in the book and Nellie…"

"Now, Tim, let's not start that again."

"But don't you think it's funny?"

"Not particularly. Ernest does Frobisher shows. It's a break getting my dress there. I like his stuff."

"Maggie, can I go with you tomorrow?"

"Darling, I didn't know you went in for that sort of thing."

"I'd just like to find out something."

"If it were to keep me company, I'd adore it, but not if you're going crawling around people with a magnifying glass."

"I promise not to goose a single goose."

"Well, all right," she said reluctantly. "Meet me there at ten."

"What about tonight? Let's celebrate."

"Haven't you a date with Libby?"

"I'll break it."

"Oh, I don't think so, darling. I'd better get a good night's sleep. I must look ravishing tomorrow. Don't forget you promised me a picture, so smile pretty at Trindler's birdie. Good night." She hung up, and I got undressed even though I knew I wouldn't be able to sleep.

I wished now I hadn't bothered to call up Libby, but I was too excited at having a job to stay in all evening by myself, so what the hell.

There was a knock on the door just as I got all my clothes off and flopped on the bed. It was Kendall again with a fistful of clippings.

"Here are the notices of *Front Page Stuff* I promised you. All the interesting parts are underlined." I knew without looking that the interesting parts were all concerned with the brilliant portrayal of one Kendall Thayer replete with pearl-gray cutaway.

"Thanks. Just throw them on the dresser and close the door softly on this exit. Make believe you're Madame X." Kendall looked a little hurt, but closed the door softly. I stretched out feeling just like Little Jack Horner with a plum on every finger.

Being an actor can be the most wonderful thing in the world...when you have a job. But when you haven't, brother, it's hell.

# CHAPTER NINE

IT WAS SEVEN FORTY-FIVE when I woke up. In twenty minutes I had showered, shaved and was on my way to the subway. I hit an express on Fourteenth Street and again Life was good to me. It wasn't till around Twenty-eighth Street that I remembered that I hadn't locked my door because Kendall hadn't given me back my keys. Not that I had anything of value in my room except the telephone, but the inhabitants of the Casbah can never resist making long-distance calls on a hot, free phone. This time I'd just have to take a chance till I got to Bergen's and could phone Kendall or the Mad Swede to lock it.

Bergen's Bar is a hole in the wall on Forty-fifth Street just off Eighth Avenue. Like a railroad car with a long bar running down the left, stopping only for the men's room, which is nothing more than an irrigated broom closet. There are some tables in a line down the right side checkered with tablecloths, a few haphazardly framed photographs of some of the customers past and present, and, of course, a jukebox.

I was fifteen minutes late. Libby was already there

sitting at the first table, right next to the jukebox, with another girl. Even though Nick had given me three tickets, it annoyed me to see that she had someone else with her. When you ask a girl to go to the theater, you don't expect her to drag along a friend. I've pulled that same trick too many times myself to enjoy being played for a sucker. She didn't know the seats were free, although with me I suppose she'd be a fool to think otherwise. And I wasn't too anxious to have an audience while I tried to pump Libby.

She says she comes from a good family in Columbus, where her father makes paper boxes and sent her to Bennington, and she's never gotten over either of them. She wears her mousy hair dank and long on the sides with bangs in front, and doesn't use any makeup except eye shadow which, for some obscure reason, she wears under her eyes. I happen to know her clothes are expensive, but she goes in for lumpy suits that look as though they were woven out of old spinach.

Her friend wasn't any more appetizing than Libby, though I must say she was better dressed in what Maggie always calls "the basic sack." She also reeked of an earlier vintage Bennington—circa when Katharine Hepburn was the dream girl—and was still sporting that scarlet, square mouth without any dip in the upper lip that Miss H. started, but had sense enough to change.

The moment I got a load of the two of them, I started trying to figure out how to cut the evening short. Libby greeted me like a spaniel and obviously expected to be kissed, so I did. She introduced me to her friend who turned out to be named Margo Shaw. I'd have laid ten to one she'd turn out to be a Margo after the first glimpse. They were drinking brandy. I settled for a rye and water and told them to hold everything, I had to phone.

I dialed the Casbah's instead of my own number and luckily Kendall answered.

"Kendall, this is Tim. Why the hell didn't you give me my keys back?"

"I'm profoundly sorry, Tim, but the simple truth of the matter is that I forgot. I'll go lock your door right this minute."

"Yeah, do that. And keep out of my drawers, too. I'll pick up the keys from you when I get back. You'll be in about midnight?"

"Most assuredly."

"Okay, then take off." I hung up and went back to the girls. We had about fifteen minutes till curtain and I couldn't waste any time. Old square-mouth didn't show any signs of blowing so I gave Libby a big smile and patted her knee under the table. "Now then. Tell me all about it." She didn't even bother to ask why I wanted to know or what I meant. Obviously it must be about Nellie as that was the only important thing that had happened to her since she had discovered eyeshadow. A swig of brandy and she was off.

"Well, it was the most amazing thing. I've just been telling Margo all about it." She turned to Margo. "Darling, you don't mind hearing it all again, do you?" As if square-mouth had any choice other than to walk out.

"Of course not, Libby. I think it's the most exciting

thing I've ever heard. You were so brave. I mean, if something like that had happened to me I don't know what I'd have…"

"Okay, okay," I said. "What happened?"

"I'm trying to tell you, Tim." More brandy, then, "I just stopped by Nellie's office to say hello—and remind her of our dinner date. And when I got to the office—"

"What time was this?" I interrupted.

"Oh, it must have been a little after eleven." At least Nellie hadn't been cooling off too long. "And the door was closed and I knocked, but, of course, there wasn't any answer. The light was on and I tried the door because I thought I might leave her a note on her desk. It was open so I went in.…" She gave a five-beat pause for effect, another swig of brandy, and to pull some hair out of her mouth that had swung in. "And what do you suppose I saw?" I allowed as how I couldn't imagine. "It was Nellie!" she said in a great rush of triumph. "Lying across her desk in a welter of blood…a welter." Okay, so if it made her feel any better to call a dribble a welter, let her. "There she was lying in a welter of blood."

"You said that. Then what happened?"

"Then everything went white." It couldn't be black like with anybody else—with her it was white. "And the next thing I knew I was screaming in Sardi's. Whatever do you suppose made me do that?"

Margo answered her, "Shock, I suppose. You said everything went white."

"Yes, that must have been it," agreed Libby. "Shock." She lowered her eyes and her white eyelids looked very strange against the smudge of black under them—almost blind.

"Okay, take it from there."

"Well, everyone rushed back up with me. And after a while, the police and press came and they made everyone clear out. All except me," she added proudly.

"What *had* happened to Nellie?"

"Oh, after they took some pictures, they flopped her back in her chair and cleaned up the place a little. And then the doctor came and they took her away in a basket."

"What did the doctor say when he examined her?" I hated having to get all the dope secondhand.

"He said it looked like she'd fainted or passed out, there was an empty gin bottle right in the desk—you know Nellie—and she'd fallen across her desk on that filing thing. You know, the one she always had on her desk." I said I knew. "Just happened to hit a vital spot and struck her heart and killed her, he guessed, without an autopsy."

"They didn't think there was anything fishy about it?"

"No. Why should they?"

"I mean did they go around spraying powder on things. You know, fingerprints?"

"I don't think so, but they might have while I was being photographed. I kind of hoped there'd be more goings on, too."

"But, darling, didn't they even look for clues?" asked Margo. Libby thought a moment.

"I don't think so, but then, I was so busy with the photographers…"

Well, I'd had it. I was just as wrong as before and really worse than Libby. She'd only made an audition of Nellie's death and I'd tried to build it up to a whole three-act melodrama.

It was time for the curtain to go up so I went over to the bar and gave Patsy the money for the drinks, making the annoying discovery that Libby and Margo had had four brandies. What she had told me wasn't worth it. I came back and helped them on with their coats.

"Would you like to go to the theater with us, Margo?" What the hell, I might just as well ask her. It wouldn't make much difference one way or the other.

"Oh, no. I couldn't," she said not too emphatically.

"You might just as well. I have three tickets, anyway. I'd just have to turn one back."

"Well, if you'll let me pay for it, I'd love to."

"Oh, no, I couldn't." Me trying to be the shy type.

"Please let me. After all, you bought the drinks, and I really barged in on Libby. It wouldn't be fair if I didn't."

"Well," I said. I hoped hesitantly. Four bucks would be almost clear profit—except for the drinks. She reached into her bag and pulled out a five-dollar bill and handed it to me.

"There, we're even. You can buy me another drink when your show opens."

"Show?" I said. "What show?"

"But aren't you in the new Frobisher show?" She turned to Libby. "Darling, I thought you told me he was in the new Frobisher show."

"Of course he is," said Libby. "It's all over town

about you and Maggie Lanson. What's the matter? You think it's bad luck to talk about it?"

"But, my God. I just found out myself an hour ago. Talk about small towns knowing everything about you."

"I wonder if they've set the understudies yet," said Libby. "You know, that might be a job for you, Margo. I'm too young for Randall, but you ought to be about right."

"Oh, no," said Margo modestly. "I couldn't do that."

"Why not?" asked Libby. "You told me you wanted to get into the theater and you might as well start somewhere. Tim will introduce you to Frobisher, won't you, Tim? It's worth a try."

"Now wait a minute," I said. "I haven't even started to rehearse, and already you've got me getting other people jobs in it. Come around after I've passed my five days, and I'll see what I can do." It didn't hurt to say that much. I certainly didn't intend to bother Frobisher with stage-struck women I hardly knew, even provided I did get the job.

"That's a date, Margo." Libby was persistent for her friends if nothing else. "Now don't forget, Tim." I said I wouldn't, but I fully intended to. She glanced at her watch. "Say, we'd better get going or we'll be late. Have you finished paying for the drinks, Tim?" I told her I had. "Oh, that reminds me. Something I forgot to tell you. Clues. About Nellie, I mean."

"Clues," I said. "What clues?"

"Asking you about the bill for the drinks must have made me think of it. Free association I guess you'd call it."

"Call what?"

"Well, they did find some money down Nellie's bazoom, if you could call that clues."

"Why, darling," said Margo. "How thrilling. You didn't tell me that."

"I just remembered it."

"Money?" I asked. "How much money?"

"It was just some she was going to pay a bill with. It was there, too."

"What was it for?"

"Two hundred and seventy-five dollars for a dress from Chez Ernest."

Chez Ernest was in the Youth and Beauty Book. An appointment that morning.

"Did you see the bill? Was it made out to Nellie?"

"Oh, yes. I saw it and it was." That didn't mean much, either. You don't kill people for intending to pay their bills.

"Well, come on or we'll be late."

We were late, but after five minutes of the show I knew it didn't matter. Probably been better if we'd gone to a movie.

Lucille Blake's latest tumbril was a high comedy. You can always tell by the terrace in the back of the set. Nick Stein had done well on the seats, and when they're free it isn't considered cricket to walk out and you're supposed to clap a lot at the end, so I got ready to sit through it.

I started thinking over what Libby had said, which, God knows, wasn't much. Nellie was certainly getting fancy in her old age laying out two hundred and seventy-five bucks for a new dress. I nudged Libby, who, still keeping an eye on the stage, twisted an ear in my direction.

"Do you remember ever seeing Nellie in any other dress but that old moss job she always wore?"

"What?" she whispered and I repeated it. "No, I don't think I have. Isn't Miss Blake divine?"

Miss Blake wasn't divine. She was tired and old and frightened. She played with such desperate determination that you felt she must have some of her own money in the show—which she had. I was relieved when it was over.

We put Margo in a cab and I started walking Libby over to Madison where she lived.

"Timmy, I hope you didn't mind too much about Margo barging in like that?"

"Who is she? I've never seen her around before. She go to Bennington with you?"

"No, she's a friend of Ted Kent's, I think. He introduced me to her this afternoon." Any friend of Ted Kent's is no friend of mine. "She's just been divorced or something and wants to act. I think she might do for Randall's understudy and it wouldn't hurt you to introduce her to Frobisher."

"But I keep telling you, I haven't started work myself yet."

"You're just being superstitious and besides, you promised. She is a good type. Why just this afternoon I took her along to the tryouts for the Equity Library shows, you know, those things they're putting on so agents and people can see you, and Vince Wagner offered her Rosalind in *As You Like It* the minute she walked into the room. But like a dope she said she wasn't ready for Shakespeare yet even though that was the lead. Vince, the louse, said I wasn't the type."

"I see no reason to encourage frustrated people to take to the theater as a cure for divorce."

"I don't see why she's any different from Maggie."

"Well, you better take another look, and besides, it's none of your goddamned business about Maggie."

"You don't need to snap my head off."

"I'm sorry, Libby, but I've had a bad day."

"I'm sorry, too. I didn't mean to say that about Maggie." We reached her hotel. "Why don't you come up for a drink."

"Won't Margo be jealous?"

"You can go to hell." She ran into the lobby.

I bought the next morning's *News* and *Mirror* in the subway station and inside was a story about Nellie with a completely unrecognisable cut of her that must have been all of fifteen years old. The stories in both the papers were about the same. Death was accidental as a result of falling on the spindle...alcohol had been found in her brain and she was known to have been susceptible to heart attacks. Nothing I didn't already know. But what did puzzle me was that the time of death was set between eight and nine-thirty a.m. Nellie had never in her life been known to be in her office before ten o'clock at the very earliest and what's more she was warm when I took her pulse and the blood was still oozing out of her. I had learned enough about blood in the army to know there was something screwy somewhere. Who was kidding who?

I was still trying to figure that one out when I opened the front door of the Casbah. Jan, Helga the housekeeper's little boy, was sitting on the hall stairs playing with something in his hand. I couldn't see what it was. There weren't any messages for me in the pigeon holes just inside the door so I started upstairs.

"Hello, Jan. What have you got there?" Jan looked at me gravely. He was about four years old and one of the most angelic-looking children I've ever seen. And one of the dirtiest. He held out a cupped hand to me and I started to shake it thinking that was what he wanted. The moment I closed my hand over his tiny one he let out a terrific scream that scared the pants off of me. I let go in a hurry. "What's the matter, Jan? I wasn't going to hurt you." His scream stopped just as suddenly as it began and he started groping around on the floor as though he'd dropped something. I got down on my knees and started to help him search, but I couldn't see anything. "What is it, Jan? What did you lose?"

"Nana," he said, feverishly groping around on the floor. "You made me drop Nana." I couldn't see anything that looked like a Nana even allowing for baby talk.

"Who is Nana?"

Suddenly he smiled and very gently he put his cupped hand, knuckles down, on the floor and then very carefully raised it up for me to see. "Nana. She's my friend." His grimy little hand was absolutely empty. I began to feel a tickle at the back of my neck. He slowly moved his hand to his chest and started to pet nothing with his other hand about five inches from his cupped one, the way you might pet a baby rabbit. I took it that Nana was very, very small.

"Isn't it a little late for you and Nana to be up?" I could play along with a gag.

"Mummy has a friend with her," he replied solemnly, not missing a stroke on Nana. Helga frequently had friends, and since she lived in only one room, renting all the rest, it appeared that Jan and Nana would have a long, long play together if I knew Helga.

"Well, good night, Jan." I started up the stairs.

"Say good-night to Nana," he said, holding up his palm again. I dutifully said good-night to Nana and went on upstairs, shaking my head.

I knocked on Kendall's room to get my key, but there was no answer. And the bum had promised he'd be in when I got back. I tried my door and sure enough he had had sense enough to lock it. No telling where the old lush would be trying to promote drinks now, so I called down for Jan and he came trotting up the stairs, both hands empty this time.

"What did you do with Nana, Jan?" He smiled that secret smile that kids have.

"Nana's gone." She apparently could be turned on and off at will.

"Listen, Jan. My door is locked and I haven't got my key. Would you go ask your mother for the pass key?" He just stood there. "Have you got that? Pass key."

"Mummy would be mad at me." I didn't intend to sit on the stairs all night, too, friend or no friend.

"No, she won't, Jan. Mummy will understand. Tell her it's for Tim. She'll give it to you." Jan shook his head violently. "I'll give you ten cents." His face lit up at that.

"I know where Mummy keeps other key."

"What other key?"

"Gimme ten cents." He was learning fast. I handed him the dime and he took off like Moody's goose down the stairs. In a few seconds he was back and presented me with a key.

"Where did you get this? Mummy give it to you?" He smiled his little smile.

"Secret."

The key fit and I opened my door and gave the key back to him and he ran downstairs again.

I wondered if Jan or Nana know how to make long-distance phone calls.

## CHAPTER TEN

ERNEST, THE OWNER OF that elegantly exclusive gray and smoky-mirrored dress shop, Chez Ernest, used to be a shiny-haired nightclub dancer until he got a little short in the wind and started to bloat. His one-of-a-kind designs are sort of a cross between Valentina and Adrian—line and texture in what I always thought were remarkably dirty colors. I've never seen one of his things, outside of blacks or whites, that had an honest-to-God normal color in it. The greens look like verdigris on an old roof and the yellows and reds something he's found out behind a hospital. But the women love it and think he shrieks with chic.

At ten the next morning, after my sitting with Trindler the photographer, the shop was empty, but at the back, through a partly open door, I could hear Jenny Pittenger's foghorn voice, so I went in.

Maggie and Jenny and Ernest were draped around the floor of Ernest's office like a bunch of bung-hole buddies looking at huge watercolor dress sketches spread out on the carpet. There were coffee cups beside them and Ernest handed me one as soon as I came in. I took off my coat and hat and threw them on a couch and joined the others on the floor.

"Good for you, darling." Maggie smiled at me. "Didn't think you'd make it. How were the photographs?"

"If the amount of fussing with lights means anything, they should be sensational." I said hello to Jenny and Ernest.

"My God!" Jenny stared at me through her thick hornrimmed glasses. "Little Sir Horror! What the hell are you doing up at this hour? Thought you were strictly an evening artist."

"Frobisher's making an honest man of me. Didn't Maggie tell you? I'm replacing someone in this new little turkey you're working on."

"Well, things are bad all over." And Jenny went back to shuffling sketches.

She was one of the rudest people in the world, but you couldn't be mad at her. She wasn't nasty, she just had the embarrassing habit of saying what she thought. I first met Jenny about eight years ago when I was an usher at her wedding. She'd been almost pretty then, at least pretty enough to get married because her family didn't have any money, but her marriage didn't take so she had a career instead of babies. She was a good designer, too, and had gotten to be top-flight the hard way. After staffing for years with Mielziner, during the war she started getting jobs on her own when most of the established scene designers were playing camouflage in the army.

With a snort Jenny tossed the sketches aside. "Look, Ernie, my little waltz, this is all crap and you know it.

Reach down in that marsupial pouch of yours and get up something decent. This elderly blond angel on my left is supposed to be attractive, not Electra's understudy."

"But, darling Jenny, those are the best I have." He began picking up the scattered sketches. He held one at arm's length. "What's the matter with this one?"

"If you don't know, dearie, I'm not going to tell you. Come on now, break out the ones you've been saving for Hope Hampton. We're your pals, see? Come on, give."

"But, Jenny, that's all I have."

"Then there's only one thing to do. Get out your little drawing pad, Mazurka, and create."

I could see this wasn't going to help me complete my mission so I got up and wandered around the office.

"Ernie, where do you keep copies..." I started to ask.

"Don't say that word," screamed Ernie. Jenny roared.

"I'm sorry. I mean where do you keep sketches of dresses you've done recently. Or don't you make one for every dress?"

"Of course I do," Ernie said over his shoulder. "They're in that portfolio by the desk." He started slashing at an enormous sketch pad with a soft pencil. I found the portfolio and leafed through the sketches. There were hundreds, but, fortunately, on the back they all had the names of the clients who had bought them, and Nellie's name was on the back of four.

So it was true. But when did Nellie ever wear them? Three of the four were mostly a peculiar shade of dirty magenta that set my teeth on edge. I pulled out one of the sketches and carried it over to Maggie.

"Look, Maggie. What about this one? Don't you think this would be nice?" She took one look at it and started to say something. I winked at her and she reluctantly picked up the cue.

"Well, yes. Look, Jenny. What's the matter with this one?"

"Crap!" said Jenny, but she began to study it, too. "Still if you like it, Mag. After all, you're going to wear it. I wouldn't, but it's not too bad with the set."

"Bad with the set or good with the set," said Ernie, "you are not going to wear that dress, darling. That model has been sold and I don't copy my own models. I leave that to others," he said loftily.

"It's just too damned bad about you," said Jenny. "That's the one we're going to have. Who got it, anyway?" She turned over the sheet and read the name on the back. "Nellie Brant? Not that old flesh peddler? Thought she was dead."

"Now that doesn't prove a thing, Timmy," said Maggie before I even opened my mouth.

"Doesn't prove what?" asked Jenny suspiciously.

"Oh, nothing," I said. "Maggie and I just had a little bet."

"Is that really who this was for, Ernie?" asked Maggie. "You're not just making it up?"

"If you let a bag like that wear this little job," said Jenny, "you're dumber than I thought. What did she want—a stylish dress to be buried in?"

Ernie snatched the sketch away from Jenny and popped it back into the portfolio.

"It so happens it was for her niece."

"What does she look like, Ernie?" I asked.

"I've never met her. She lives in a one-night-stand called Hopkinsville, Kentucky, and I've done several things for her in the last couple of years."

"Kind of letting the bars down, aren't you?" said Jenny. "Didn't know you were in the mail-order business yet. Do send me a catalog. They're so handy." This stung him.

"As a rule I build my models on the client, but Nellie is an old friend and I made an exception."

"Do you do it from measurements?" asked Jenny sweetly. "Or do you just add water?"

"It so happens she is a perfect model size." He eyed Jenny's bulk. "Which of course you wouldn't know anything about." Jenny slapped him on the back.

"Okay, two-step. You win."

After a good deal of name-calling a sketch and samples were finally decided on. A sulphur yellow and what was called "greige" was it. Maggie put her foot down on any dirty reds or greens and I backed her up. Ernie promised it would be finished in time for the opening in Wilmington.

"See that it is," said Jenny darkly. "Or else! And don't forget my cut, either, you old miser, and now hows about a drink?" Ernie pushed a button and a bar appeared out of the wall. "Come on, kiddies, let's get stinking."

"We've got to be at rehearsal in fifteen minutes," said Maggie. "Some other time. Call me and let's have lunch."

"I'll do that." Jenny poured herself a generous belt.

We said goodbye to Ernie and left him looking appre-hensively at Jenny, who had already started on her second drink.

I waited till we flagged a cab before I asked Maggie what she thought of the sketches I had discovered.

"Under that moss of Nellie's must have beaten a heart of gold," was her comment.

"But two hundred and seventy-five per, just for a niece. Does that sound like Nellie?"

"Don't tell me you're trying to find something sinister in that?"

"But can you see those scabby reds and poison greens in the local Hopkinsville juke joint?"

"We all have our little weaknesses."

But it still didn't seem in character for Nellie, who had been the hardest woman with a dollar I'd ever met.


No matter how many plays you have been in before, you always get a few butterflies at your first rehearsal of a new one. You take off your hat very carefully so you won't mess up your hair and you wonder if your shoes are shined enough and your trousers are still pressed and you keep wiping off the palms of your hands so they won't be like wet fish when you shake hands with people.

The Lyceum Theater stage door is on Forty-sixth Street although the entrance to the theater itself is on Forty-fifth. Maggie and I didn't say anything as I helped her out of the cab and opened the stage door.

We walked down a narrow hall and I opened the door leading onto the stage proper and we tiptoed in. The set from the show that was still playing at the Lyceum was up and the rehearsal was on. We could hear voices as we walked around the back of the set, stepping over cables and dodging props. It was very dark, just a few leaks from the big, bare work light hanging in the middle of the stage. We groped around to the proscenium arch and looked in. Frobisher was sitting on a chair in front of the footlights directing a scene. He saw us and motioned us to wait. I wanted a cigarette, but no one else seemed to be smoking and some theaters are stuffy about it backstage. In a couple of minutes Frobisher told the cast to take a break and came to us. We shook hands and I was glad mine was comparatively dry.

He was still looking tired, but everyone gets nervy as opening night creeps up. He'd probably been up every night helping with the rewriting.

He said how glad he was to see us and asked us to come with him while he introduced us to the rest of the company. Just before we followed him out on the stage, Maggie and I shook hands behind his back.

It was a good cast Frobisher had assembled. Small, only ten counting Maggie and me, but you knew who all of them were, if not personally, at least by name. Miss Randall, the lead, had been starred for years. Paul Showers who played her husband was on loan from Hollywood and none of them was working for coffee and cakes. I wondered how much the actor I had replaced got. I began to wish I had held out for a hundred and fifty, but it was too late now. At least I wouldn't have to pay any commission. It was odd to think that if Nellie wasn't dead I would be giving her five per cent every week. She had agented all the others.

Frobisher started right in with the last act and since the play had been in rehearsal for two weeks, even though our parts were small, Maggie and I had a lot of catching up to do. It was three o'clock before we realized it and Frobisher quietly announced that because of Nellie's funeral we would break for the rest of the afternoon, but an evening rehearsal would be held at his Sutton Place apartment promptly at seven-thirty.

Greg Moulton, the stage manager, told Maggie and me that from now on, Mr. Frobisher wanted us to attend every rehearsal because there might be some skipping back and forth in the acts.

There was still half an hour before the ceremony so Maggie and I walked up Broadway to the Henderson Funeral Home at Sixty-eighth Street where the services were to be held. We stopped off for a couple of swallows on the way and as it turned out, almost everyone else at the funeral had had the same idea.

## CHAPTER ELEVEN

WHEN WE GOT TO THE funeral home, except for the fact that it was Sixty-eighth Street instead of Forty-fourth, the crowd looked like the sidewalk in front of Sardi's at rush hour. I expect Nellie would have been pleased at such a good house.

Kendall Thayer was there in fine fettle and his courtly bow aimed in my general direction almost threw him on his face.

A cab pulled up and Jenny poured out. She, from the looks of her, had just this minute left Ernie and his sliding bar.

"Darlings!" she screamed when she saw us. "Isn't this heaven? All this crush makes me feel like a bud again." And she promptly collapsed against Maggie. Between the two of us, we managed to keep her from slumping into the gutter.

The crowd was jamming the doors and just ahead of us were Ted Kent, Libby and old square-mouth Margo. I certainly didn't want to sit with those three and if we went in now we might have to. I still was feeling a little guilty about charging Margo for that ticket last night and, also, I didn't want to give her a chance to remind me of that understudy job again.

"Let's wait a minute, Maggie."

"But I can't hold Jenny up much longer," Maggie complained. We propped Jenny against the wall and lit cigarettes, but my unfavorite three evidently decided to let the rest of the crowd get in first, too, and they elbowed their way out on the sidewalk again and, of course, couldn't help seeing us.

Ted *darlinged* Maggie and, much to my annoyance, kissed her. Libby just pretended I didn't exist. She was sore, I guess, about my crack the other night. But not old square-mouth Margo. To my astonishment she threw her arms around me and kissed me. Maybe she was just doing it to make Ted mad for the way he kissed Maggie, but whatever her motives, it was one of the busiest kisses I have ever been on the other end of.

It startled me so I almost jumped. I thought Maggie was too taken up with Ted to notice, she was standing with her back to me, but without stopping her conversation with Ted, she reached in her purse and pulled out a handkerchief and put it in my hand. There wasn't anything else to do but shamefacedly wipe the lipstick off my mouth as she had intended me to do. Maybe I'd been wrong about Libby and Margo being an item.

"I had such a good time last night," Margo said. "I do hope you'll forgive me for barging in like that on you and Libby."

"That's okay," I said. Just then Jenny started sliding down the wall to the sidewalk. Now that Ted was here he might as well work. "Help me get Jenny inside, will you, Ted? If we can get her set somewhere she ought to be okay." He took her other arm and we started to lift her up. Jenny opened one bleary eye.

"Whassa matter?"

"Come on. Stand up, Jenny." I said. "We're going inside."

"Whaffor?"

"You remember Nellie's funeral?" She struggled to her feet.

"Oh, yes. Gotta see Nellie's dress."

"What's the matter with her?" asked Ted.

"Gotta see old Nellie in Ernie's dress. Ole queen of the blood suckers in Ernie's stylish dress."

"It isn't Nellie's dress," I explained patiently. "It's her niece's."

"Then gotta see ole Nellie's niece in Ernie's stylish dress." At last she was vertical and the five of us got her inside where another drunk latched on to our happy little band. Kendall Thayer. This was getting to be too much of a good thing and I was all for dumping Jenny and grabbing Maggie and getting the hell out, but Kendall was demanding introductions to the three girls and there wasn't much I could do. I know from experience that when Kendall starts trotting out that roguish matinee-idol routine you have no choice.

He must have had a breath like a serpent for Margo, unto whom, luckily for Maggie, he fastened first. She made no bones about the way she felt and held her handkerchief up to her nose the whole time he was talking to us. We managed to shake him at last and find seats in the rear.

It was twenty years since I had been to a real sit-down funeral. I didn't like it then and the minute I sat down, I wished I was somewhere else. The organ music and the smell of flowers banked around the coffin brought back things I didn't particularly want brought back.

I must admit Nellie's friends had done well by her. There seemed to be a great many flowers. The casket was in front of a little altar and a minister or preacher…a man in vestments, anyway, was standing by it. The chapel was packed with people. Nellie was playing to S.R.O. and most of the audience acted as though they had just stopped by from a cocktail party. After you got used to the smell of flowers you started noticing the alcohol base like a cheap perfume. Kendall had found a seat well up front not far from Frobisher. The whole thing seemed more like an Equity meeting with a sprinkling of producers and agents than a funeral. Luckily Jenny had lapsed into a snoring stupor. I thought it better to let her snore than to wake her up and take a chance on her that way.

Maggie was getting tight. I could tell by the way she kept pushing her hair back across her face. It's a gesture I know well and means that she is well on the way. The drinks we'd had on the way were beginning to hit me, too, and I couldn't focus very clearly on what was going on. I remember the minister getting up and mumbling something and the next thing I knew Kendall was standing beside him. He seemed to have taken over and there was no chance to avoid hearing those resonant tones. He was giving a performance. Not being awfully up on my funerals, I wasn't aware it was considered a yes thing to have some of the audience get up and say a few well-chosen words like Brutus in the one time I had a fling at Shakespeare. But it didn't seem quite right. Kendall was actually starting out with a paraphrase of that "Friends, Romans, Countrymen" chestnut. The minister looked too startled to do anything about it and Kendall did as neat a job of upstaging as I have ever seen.

"Friends, Producers, Equity Members." He was taking it big. "I come not only to praise Nellie, but to bury her." He brushed away a tear, undoubtedly pure alcohol. "We are saying farewell to not only a great friend, a great little agent, but a great artist, as well. I remember when she was with me in *Front Page Stuff,* such brilliance! Such charm! Such vitality! Perhaps some of you remember that unforgettable table scene we had together. I was playing Lord Washburn and she mistook me for the butler. That scene took all the notices as perhaps you recall. In playing that scene for forty weeks we found the true theater and I knew I was right in turning my back on the Hollywood gold where I had been so long as a star with Fox Films." The crowd at first was too surprised to do anything but sit dumbly—now they started to titter. Jenny pulled herself up out of her slump and peered around like a walrus looking for fish.

"Crap," she snorted and immediately went back to sleep. People were laughing now, and Mr. Frobisher somehow guided Kendall back to his seat and once more the startled minister began, but it was too late to get back the audience's attention. Everyone started talking among themselves and a few people actually got up and went over to talk to friends standing at the back.

The minister doggedly kept going. He had so many sides to his part and he was determined to say them regardless.

I was feeling embarrassed and tried to shush a few of the noisier ones, but no one paid any attention to me. I hoped the minister would be through or give up pretty soon. Maggie and I stood up. I was feeling none too steady.

"Maggie," I said. "Let's go."

"What about Jenny?"

"Leave her lie. She'll be all right...." Under the circumstances that seemed the only thing we could do. It would take a half-pound block of TNT to budge her. "You follow me. I'll run interference for you." We had almost broken through the line of scrimmage and made the door when Kendall clipped me from behind.

"Tim...Tim...I want to talk to you." Well, I didn't want to talk to old serpent's-breath again. Now or ever.

"Go on. Beat it, Kendall. I've nothing to say to you after that performance you just gave." I savagely jerked my arm out of his fingers. "Blow!"

"But, Tim, this is important." I almost hit him.

"Beat it, I tell you." Maggie and I started up again and this time I was blocked head-on by Ted Kent.

"I was looking for you, Tim. You're on." He started back to the front of the chapel.

"Hey, wait a minute," I called after him. "I'm on what?"

"You dope. You're supposed to help tote Nellie's barge." And then I remembered that Frobisher had asked me to be a pallbearer and I couldn't very well not, under the circumstances.

"I've got to go bear a pall," I told Maggie. "See you at your place afterward." I elbowed my way down the aisle and grabbed one of the silver casket handles. Ted, Mr. Frobisher and some other juveniles around town were already spotted at the other handles.

Someone started to sing "For She's a Jolly Good Fellow" but was quickly discouraged. That was too much even for this crowd. The minister with one horrified look disappeared through a little door. Jenny came staggering up, flailing her arms jut as Mr. Frobisher gave the signal and we hoisted the casket.

Alive, Nellie was no featherweight, and dead, she hadn't shed a pound. I could feel the sweat breaking out on my forehead. A glance at the other pallbearers told me they weren't having any better time of it than I was.

The rest of the audience filed out into the street after us. We managed to ease the casket into the waiting hearse. Mr. Frobisher said we would ride to the station in his car, which was parked right behind the hearse. After we had run back into the chapel and grabbed our coats and hats, we started to pile into the car. I got in first.

Sitting over in the corner of the backseat was a girl, dressed in black, crying noisily into a sodden handkerchief. Mr. Frobisher got in after me. Ted sat up front with the chauffeur and another juvenile and the other two drew the jump seats. I had the sensation that any minute the crowd would begin throwing rice and old shoes at us.

"Gentlemen," said Mr. Frobisher. "I'd like to present Miss Mary Ellen Taylor, Miss Brant's niece." This brought on a great burst of sobs as he spieled off our names.

"I think they were all the most horrid people I ever heard of." She was slightly muffled by the handkerchief mashed against her face. Frobisher tried to comfort her, but she would have none of it. "Carryin' on like that with poor old Aunt Nellie lyin' right there." The accent was pure "Uncle Tom." "I hope something awful happens to every one of them. And that terrible old man that did all that talkin'. Didn't he know he wasn't supposed to do that?" Kendall Thayer. "I do believe some of those people were *drunk.*" This grim thought sent her into even louder sobs. I still couldn't get it straight.

"Are you really Nellie's niece? I mean her *only* niece?" A red-rimmed eye glared at me around the gray handkerchief.

"'Course I am. The only kin poor old Aunt Nellie had in the whole world. She was the finest, most generous aunt in creation—" And off she was again.

The rumpled black suit and dusty felt hat she was wearing would have sent Ernie screaming for a burnt feather. I gave up!

It was getting hot in the car and I must have dozed off, for when I came to we were parked outside the baggage room at Penn Station. The pallbearers bore

Nellie once more, this time into the baggage room, and since there didn't seem to be anything else to do, we got back in the car, smoked and waited for Mr. Frobisher, who, with Miss Taylor, was arranging for tickets. None of us said very much. Juveniles as a rule don't have much in common, and Ted and I, who certainly couldn't be called juveniles, didn't even bother to try.

While we waited, I tried to figure out the angles, but I didn't get anywhere. Nellie couldn't have had a second niece, or, if she did, Little Mary Ellen would surely have known about her and there was no particular point in lying to me about it. Something was strictly not on the up and up!

# CHAPTER TWELVE

WHEN I GOT TO MAGGIE'S apartment, she was just getting ready to take a bath and opened the door in a great white bathrobe with her hair pinned up on top of her head. She looked about sixteen.

"What took you so long?"

"I was seeing Nellie home. Mr. Frobisher dropped me off here."

"My, my. Aren't we coming up in the world? Did he buy your dinner for you, too?"

"No. But it might interest you to know he offered to."

"I'm that impressed. Well, call up Schrafft's and have them send something over with lots of coffee. We've got to be in shape for rehearsal tonight. Why don't you lie down while I take my bath, then you can have one, too. You could probably use one after that shindig. Did you ever see anything so disgusting? Actors are really awful people, aren't they?"

She headed for the bathroom. I followed her into the bedroom and stripped down to my shorts and lay on her bed. She started splashing around in the bathtub. Clouds of steam were coming out the door.

"If the bath salts get you down," she called, "just open a window. I need some after that." She started to close the door. Her bath salts even matched her perfume. So that's how she did it. It smelled warm and steamy and good.

"Leave the door open. I want to talk." She did and I could hear her getting in the tub. I lay back and looked at the ceiling.

"I met Nellie's niece," I said finally.

"Really? What was she like."

"A flower of the ole Sooth. And she would never wear one of Ernie's dresses, either. I'll bet anything in the world on that."

"Well, so what? People have lots of nieces. Maybe Nellie had one a little more glamorous tucked away somewhere."

"'I'm all the kith and kin poah li'l ole Aunt Nellie had in this great big horrid world.' And I quote li'l Missy Mary Ellen Taylor. Now will you admit it?"

"I'll admit nothing of the kind and what's more I'm bored with the whole business. Have you ordered dinner yet?" I told her I hadn't. "Well, do it, then. It takes forever to get here. We haven't got all night, you know." The water was gurgling out of the tub. I reached for the phone by her bed.

"What's the number?"

"Volunteer something. For God's sake look it up."

"Where do you keep the book?"

"Oh, never mind, I'll do it. You were just waiting for me to, anyway." She came out of the bathroom tying the cord of the big white bathrobe. "You are the laziest person

I've ever known. Go ahead, the bathroom's all yours." She sat on the side of the bed and pulled the telephone book out from a little cupboard in the bedside table.

"I know, if it had been a snake it would have bit me." She started thumbing through the directory. Little beads of moisture still clung to her face. Her forehead was wrinkled with concentration. I reached up and smoothed it out with my thumb.

"Oh, stop it. Now you made me lose my place. U comes before S or after? I never can remember."

I pulled out the pin that held the pile of hair up and it tumbled down around her shoulders. Part of it fell in front of her eyes and she pushed it aside with an irritated gesture.

I shoved the telephone book out of her hands and pulled her back on the bed and kissed her. She didn't react one way or the other. I let her go and she sat up and picked up the telephone book and started looking through it again. I felt a little annoyed.

"What's the matter?"

"Nothing."

"Well, why so coy?"

"I'm not being coy."

"Well, you're certainly trying to be something."

"I'm not trying to be anything at all, but I just don't like you feeling that you have to earn that hundred bucks with me. Save your energy, you may need it when the hundred's gone."

"That's a hell of a thing to say." I sat up on the other side of the bed.

"You know it's true."

"Of all the snide remarks! What's gotten into you lately? You've been acting funny for the last three days."

"*I've* been acting funny! What about you with all this hocus-pocus about Nellie? You don't realize how dull it is. It may have been amusing at first, but to keep on and on with a thing… I really think you ought to go see a doctor.… I mean it, seriously. I don't think you've got all your buttons. First, this Nellie fixation and now getting in a pet just because I don't happen to want to play footsie with you."

"Well, you can take your lousy hundred bucks and you know what you can do with it." I started to get up.

"I know, I know. If you had your pants on you'd fling the money in my face. But you haven't got your pants on, as a matter of fact, you look damn silly standing there trying to be wounded dignity in your underwear. Now be a good boy and go take your bath and I'll order some food and let's forget all about it. You can even use some of my bath salts."

"Thank you, I'm sure." I stalked into the bathroom as well as you can stalk in bare feet on a thick carpet. I made myself purposely not think about what Maggie had said and, for spite, I used a lot of her bath salts and got out of the tub smelling to high heaven and feeling wonderful and hungry as a horse. Maggie was dressed when I came back to the bedroom and was finishing putting on her face.

"I'm sorry I was such a louse," I said.

"I'm sorry, too. It's none of my damn business what you do."

"That wasn't why I wanted to kiss you, though." The door buzzer buzzed.

"There's the food. Now hurry up and get dressed. We haven't got much time." I got dressed and when I came into the living room she had opened all the cartons and set the table with china from the kitchenette. The table was in front of the couch and she had lit the fire in the little white marble fireplace. It was nice and the food was good; no whipped cream, which, for Schrafft's, is unusual. I lit her cigarette when we were finished. I lit mine and we settled back on the couch. There were still fifteen minutes before we had to leave for Sutton Place. I felt contented and tried a smoke ring without much luck.

"Timmy."

"Uh-huh." I was concentrating on another smoke ring.

"Why don't you try being respectable?"

"What do you mean, respectable? I resent that."

"You know what I mean. You can't keep on this way forever."

"What way?" I knew perfectly well what she meant.

"Well, all this helling around. Your looks won't last forever."

"I intend to grow old gracefully, distinguished like Lewis Stone."

"What if your hair falls out?"

"Boyer's not doing so bad. Why all this sudden interest in my follicles? Are you getting to that age where you want to do Good Works and reform me? What about you?"

"Oh, I don't count. I've already had a life of sorts. Now I'm just waiting around."

"What for?"

"Not for anything special…just waiting. But I've got some money…at least I don't have to worry about that. I know you do."

"Maybe I'll get a picture contract. You never can tell."

"Don't you think if you were going to get one you'd have had it before now? You've been around for ten years."

"They're just waiting for me to mellow." I didn't like any part of this conversation. It was all right for me to ask myself these things, but not for other people. "You're waiting, I'm waiting. At least I know what I'm waiting for. Now let's talk about something else. How did we get on this gruesome subject, anyway?" I poured out the last of the coffee. I didn't feel up to going into the ramifications of Operation Hollywood.

"Are you going to marry Diana?" she asked suddenly.

"Good God, no. Whatever made you think of that?"

"I don't know. It might be a good idea."

"Well, in the first place she hasn't asked me." Maggie burst out laughing before I realized how silly what I had said must have sounded.

"Maybe she's the old-fashioned type and wants to *be* asked."

"That would be a hell of a note, me married to Diana."

"I think it's a fine idea.… Why not? She's rich, isn't she? She's not still married to that dreary poop, is she?"

"No."

"Well, then," she said triumphantly, "there you are! They do wonderful jobs on teeth out in Hollywood. I still don't see why with all that money she hasn't done something about them before. I believe they file them down to little points."

"That sounds silly."

"And then they stick caps on and you can't tell the difference. Of course, I do believe you can't eat anything tougher than Clapps Baby Food but she could afford to lose some weight, and I'm sure it would help her skin."

"Never mind about Diana's skin."

"I know, you found a Rose in No-Man's Land."

"Don't be silly. We've got to get going. It's a fifteen-minute walk."

"Sit back. I'll blow us to a cab. I'm fascinated with your life."

"What do you think I am? An apartment to be done over?"

"I'm worried about you. If you're not going to get married, you've got to get a job."

"I've got a job. Remember? And it starts in twenty minutes."

"I mean a real job."

"What sort of a job could I get? I don't know anything."

"You could sell something."

"What? Fuller brushes?"

"No, bonds, insurance. People do."

"Other people maybe…not me. I wouldn't be any good at it."

"You might be a G-man. God knows you're trying hard enough to be, in an amateur way. You could have fearful fun raising merry old hell with the police. Every

time someone dies of heart failure you could make a big
murder case out of it."

"You still don't believe anything is fishy about
that, do you?"

"I know what you're going to say. Just because we
thought we found a sketch of a dress that Ernie said was
for Nellie's niece and it wasn't. That doesn't prove a thing.
Promise me one thing, will you? It's for your own good."

"What is it?"

"Promise first."

"Oh, don't be childish."

"I'm sorry." She didn't say anything for a minute.
"But I really am worried about you," she continued
doggedly. "You've got a job now, and if you don't bitch
it up it'll be a decent run and you can get a little ahead.
Promise me you'll forget all about the Nellie thing until
at least opening night. Then I don't care what you do.
But I want you to promise me that. I've never asked you
to do anything for me before, but I've got a feeling
you're talking yourself into a fine little cell at Bellevue.
Promise?"

She was right. I had been a little cracked on the
subject. There wasn't one tangible thing to prove that
Nellie's death hadn't been on the up and up. It could
have been a typo in the papers about the time of death.
Out of the thousand characters that walk along Forty-
fourth Street, one of them didn't want to be bothered
with Bertha and her autograph book. Bobby LeB. might
have been an old friend from Hopkinsville whose train
was late for all I knew. Nellie may have just called

someone her niece, the way people are called uncle or aunt when they really are no relation at all. All my rushing about the last two days did seem pretty pointless and mostly just an effort to justify to myself and Maggie my acting like a road-company Hamlet the day I went to call on Nellie.

"Okay. I promise."

"Thank you," said Maggie. "You may kiss me now, if you like."

I liked.

## CHAPTER THIRTEEN

THE REHEARSAL THAT NIGHT was very elegant and I felt terribly, terribly.

Frobisher's Sutton Place apartment was a duplex and the two-storey living room seemed almost as big as the Lyceum stage. Greg had already pulled the furniture around to make the set. The room was all very *Town and Country,* gray-green walls and lots of heavy goldish drapes. The original of the Birnbaum cartoon of Frobisher from the *New Yorker* profile was keeping company on the walls with two Degas and a Lautrec. The cartoon was an uncanny likeness with just a few wirelike lines—the naked-face look with no eyebrows. I should think Birnbaum would be very pleased if he knew.

One end of the room had a terrace overlooking the East River and when they weren't on, most of the cast spent the evening standing out there. It should have been chilly in February, but with the big glass doors open, enough heat came out so that it was as warm as the living room. Little tugs glided by and the great bridge loomed and winked its lights. The Sunshine Biscuit sign was even pretty. Maggie and I, who were out there first, played a little game—seeing how many of the cast within a count of ten after they stepped on the terrace *didn't* say when they saw the view, "Why it looks just like a backdrop."

Not one of them missed.

The living room itself had a "done" look as though some scene designer like Jones or Chaney was responsible for it. Maybe this was some of Jenny's fine Italian hand. Effective and comfortable, but you had a feeling that if you went through one of the doors and turned around, the wall would be plain canvas flats with lashed-together wooden battens on the back.

After rehearsal, a butler straight from Lonsdale appeared with drinks and we all sat around for an hour and gossiped about the funeral, other plays, performances and people. It was extremely pleasant. Frobisher was a good host and Miss Randall was amusing about Hollywood and everyone was in a glow of well-being when we got ready to leave. Maggie left with Miss Randall, who would share her cab as far as the Gotham where she was stopping. I told them to go on. I was going to take the subway to the Village. I had left my coat and hat on an enormous flat-topped desk that took up one corner of the living room and I went to pick it up. It was certainly an impressive desk. Hollywood couldn't do much better. Lots of tooled leather things, blotters and penholders and a matching leather frame of a photograph. I picked up the photograph and looked at it. It was of a woman, hair parted in the middle and drawn severely back over the ears, dark shining eyes in a strong face.

"My wife," said a voice over my shoulder. I turned and Mr. Frobisher himself was standing beside me, smiling at me.

"She's very lovely. I think I must have seen her on the stage."

"No. My wife was never on the stage."

"Really? But I'm sure I've seen her somewhere."

"I think that's hardly possible. She died thirty years ago in California."

"I'm sorry, sir, I didn't know." Mr. Frobisher took the photograph from me and stared at it for a few moments then put it gently back on the desk. The breeze from the open terrace windows ruffled some papers while I was putting on my coat and Mr. Frobisher set a gold paper weight on top of them. I was struck by the curious design. "Do you mind if I look at that, sir?"

"Not at all." He handed it to me. Wrought in gold and exact in every detail was a miniature stage door. Accurate even to the electric light hooking out at the top. On the base was inscribed: "To Henry Frobisher in grateful appreciation—The Stage Door Canteen."

"I know it's a little late, sir, but I'd like to add my appreciation for what you did with the Canteen. It was a wonderful thing."

"That's very kind of you, Tim. I'm grateful you feel that way."

"And I can't tell you, sir, how sorry I was when I heard you lost your son." It didn't seem possible that pain could surge into a face so quickly. I could have kicked myself for opening my big mouth. Christ. Will I ever learn? But no. I have to be the one to rub it in. I have to put in my two cents' worth. I have to stand in front of him with all my arms and legs and tell him what a pity it was that his son got blown to bits in Normandy. I might just as well have kicked him in the teeth and been done with it.

I clumsily tried to apologize, but I don't think he even knew when I left. He just stood there, staring at his dead wife's picture.

It was a little after eleven when I, thoroughly ashamed of myself, unlocked the door to the Casbah.

There was a message from Kendall in my box to be sure and drop in and see him when I got home. Jan wasn't at his usual post on the stairs. Helga must be taking a night off to catch up on her beauty sleep. I climbed the three flights to my room and then decided to see Kendall first. I wasn't particularly sleepy and wanted someone to talk to, and also to chew him out for his disgraceful drunken episode this afternoon.

His room is on the same floor and just around the corner from mine. I knocked, but there wasn't any answer. I tried the door. It was open, and when I stuck my head in the light was on but the room was empty. Oh, well, he'd probably forgotten all about his note to me and was out trying to promote another drink. Evidently it had been a fairly profitable night in the radio business. His bed had two or three cartons of soap and some breakfast foods on it. I closed the door and walked around the corner to my own room. While I was putting the key in the lock, the door swung partway open. It made me mad, for I distinctly remembered locking it when I left that morning. But something was against it. I shoved it harder and forced it open. I switched on the lights and looked to see what had been holding the door. I took one look and just made the bathroom.

Sprawled on the floor, lying on his back, was a man's body. A shiny pool of blood was seeping under his head. His eyes were closed, but his face was mottled red like a bad birthmark, almost as though he had spilled ketchup on it. Near one of his outflung hands was a brown bottle with a bright yellow label and in spite of the bile still in my nose my room smelled like a subway toilet.

The body belonged to Kendall Thayer.

## CHAPTER FOURTEEN

YOU'D THINK BY THIS time I would be used to opening doors and finding bodies, but maybe it's something you never get used to, like opening night. The smell was the main thing that got me and as I knelt down to take Kendall's pulse I saw the odor was caused by what had been in the brown bottle—Lysol. There was a faint pulse.

What I did from then on is still rather vague. I must have yelled or pounded on the door, for a lot of people, including Helga, who was wearing a mud pack and curlers, came running. All the denizens of the Casbah must have heard me. Almost immediately the hall was filled with craning people and a great deal of shoving about. I don't know yet who sent for the ambulance and the police. Helga must have done it as soon as she looked in and saw that face. She pushed the rest of them away and shut my door. I managed to pull myself together and between us we picked Kendall up and put him on my bed. I loosened his collar and Helga got a towel and some water from the bathroom and bathed his face. The blotches had been caused by the Lysol. It was all over his face and neck and the skin was red and raw.

Mercifully, Kendall was still unconscious. He came to just before the ambulance arrived. I was reading the label on the Lysol bottle trying to find out what you did for the burns, when he started to move. He tried to claw at his face, but Helga and I held his hands down. He started thrashing his body back and forth and moaned. I couldn't make out at first what he was saying, but it got louder and louder.

"My eyes. Oh God, my eyes. My eyes." He was screaming when the doctor pounded on the door. I opened it and led him in. There was also a medic with a stretcher and a couple of policemen shooing away the crowd. The doctor took one look at Kendall and without a word opened his bag and gave him an injection. The few minutes we waited for the dope to take effect, all three of us had to hold Kendall down to keep him from clawing out his eyes and throwing himself off the bed. His eyes were open and had a milky look, like cataracts.

Gradually he quieted down and soon he was lying still, his breath whistling through his swollen lips. The doctor called in the medic and they started spreading some stuff on Kendall's face. I felt I was going to be sick again so I opened the window and leaned out, sucking in fresh air. After a while I felt that maybe I was all right and pulled my head back in the room. They had loaded him on the stretcher and were carrying him out the door. A policeman was talking to Helga. With her curlers shaking and the mud on her face already starting to crack, she looked like a badly made-up alien. The cop had a notebook and was taking down her name and story. When I heard his voice I was surprised that it wasn't Irish. It should have been with his red face and hamlike hands wrestling with the pencil. He looked very tired and his mouth was small and pursy. His voice had a whine in it.

"Someone pound on my door and say come quick something happened to Mr. Thayer in Mr. Briscoe's room," Helga was saying. "So I come quick."

The cop looked at me. "You Mr. Briscoe?"

I said I was. He asked for my full name and I gave it to him. I caught myself almost giving him my rank and army serial number, too.

"Well, go on, Mrs. Sorenson." He glanced at his book for the last name. "Then what did you do?"

"I come running up here. I was in bed already. There was poor Mr. Thayer lying on the floor. We picked him up and put him on the bed and I told another tenant to call police and ambulance." It seemed to me that the policeman ought to begin with me if he was going to question people. After all, it was my room and I had found Kendall, but it seemed to be one person at a time. "He had that Lysol stuff all over his face and I got some water and tried to wipe it off. I hope it was the right thing. And then they come and take him away."

"Has he been your tenant long, Mrs. Sorenson? This Thayer person."

"Three...four years."

"Thank you, Mrs. Sorenson." He turned to me. "Now, Mr...." He consulted his book again. "Briscoe. How did you happen to find him?"

"Well," I began. "This is my room and I unlocked the door, only it wasn't locked."

"You unlocked the door only it wasn't locked. Now just how did you do that?" I could feel myself getting more and more angry. That seemed ridiculous quibbling to me. He must have known what I meant.

"I simply mean I put my key in to unlock it but it was already open and swung in a little way and stopped when it hit Kendall's body. I pushed it open enough to get through and turned on the lights and saw him lying there. I thought at first he was dead."

"Why did you think he was dead?"

"I don't know, but he was so still and all, and then that smell…"

"The Lysol, you mean?"

"Yes. The bottle was lying on the floor," I said. "I'm afraid I got sick." He gave me an irritating smile. "When I got through being sick I came back and took his pulse and found out he was alive. I don't remember exactly what I did, but I must have yelled. Anyway, I got all those people outside the door up. Then Helga came and we did what she said and they came and took him away and that's all."

"Any idea how it happened?"

"No. I can't understand what he was doing in my room in the first place. I remembered locking my door this morning."

"Mr. Briscoe always keeps his door locked." Helga nodded a grotesque agreement to my statement. "Very particular…"

"Where was he when you found him?"

I pointed out the exact place. "His head was in the bloody place there."

"It wasn't a bad wound," said Helga. "I bathed it, too. It was just in the back of the head. Not much blood. Almost stopped bleeding."

"Now, how could he have got that?" The policeman looked around the room and his eyes fastened on my dresser. The dresser is about waist-high and has a plate-glass top that covers it completely. He examined the top of it very carefully and then pointed to one corner above where Kendall had been lying. "Yeah, you can see some blood there." We looked and there was a little blood on the corner and what looked like a few bits of Kendall's hair and skin. "This man Thayer drink much?"

"All the time." Helga was very definite about that. "All the time he drink, drink, drink. He owe me for the rent. He go hungry, but he drink."

"Well, I guess that's enough." The policeman put away his pencil and notebook. "The way I see it, he must have staggered and fallen against that dresser glass and spilled the open bottle of Lysol on himself when he fell." He was very pleased with this bit of deducting.

"But what was he doing carrying an open bottle of Lysol? I keep it in the bathroom."

"Oh, so you admit it's yours?" I said I did. "How the hell should I know what he was doing with it. Maybe he was thirsty and wanted a drink. Some of the smoke these bums drink isn't much better."

"He wasn't a bum." I don't know why I felt called upon to defend what good name Kendall may have had left.

"Okay, what do *you* call it?"

"He was an actor."

"An actor, huh? What's the difference?" I let that one pass.

"How did he get in my room, then?"

"You left the door open. The cleaning woman left the door open. How in hell should I know?"

"I never did," said Helga indignantly.

"There, you see?"

"Look, Mac. What are you trying to make out of this, a murder? The guy ain't even dead. They took him to St. Vincent's on Eleventh. I'm just trying to get enough dope for a routine report. Why don't you go ask *him* how he got in your room?" He opened the door. Some of the crowd was still hanging around out in the hall. "Okay, break it up. All over, just a little accident. Break it up." He went on downstairs. Helga followed him. A couple of the people in the hall wanted to come into my room and hear all about it, but I told them I was sick and shut the door in their faces.

I *was* sick, too. For a minute I thought of going around to St. Vincent's and seeing Kendall and getting it all straightened out, but they had given him dope and he would probably be asleep. The best thing to do would be to run down during the lunch break tomorrow. He'd be awake then and feeling a lot better and maybe I would, too.

I mopped up the blood on the floor. The bedspread also

had blood on it. I put that in the laundry bag. I even wiped off the dresser corner where he had hit his head, then I undressed and got in bed, but I didn't sleep very well.

All night long I kept waking up, hearing Kendall screaming, "My eyes... Oh God, my eyes." And I could see them, white in the red sockets, staring out at me in the dark.

# CHAPTER FIFTEEN

MY STORY CREATED QUITE a little sensation at rehearsal at the Lyceum next morning. Mr. Frobisher was late and the rest of the cast was gathered around me and I am sorry to say I was making a big thing of it.

"I remember Thayer in the old silents," said Miss Randall. "I thought he was wonderful. He was always a prince and Priscilla Barnes was the gypsy, or he was the gypsy and she was the princess. What a pity! Do you suppose he'll be blind? If any of that stuff got in his eyes I don't see how he can help it. Poor darling." Paul Showers had even worked with him in a picture.

"It was years ago, I was just a kid extra, but I'll never forget his insisting on music. Of course those were the days when you could do that sort of thing. He always had a string quartet to get him in the mood." I hadn't realized that poor old Kendall had been quite such a success as he had insisted on telling everyone.

Mr. Frobisher came onto the stage.

"Oh, Frobie," said Miss Randall.

"Sorry I'm late, people." He took off his coat. "Had to okay some furniture."

"Frobie, you remember Kendall Thayer…you know, the one you were telling about last night that made such a scene at that funeral?"

"Certainly, I'll never forget it. One of the most disgusting performances I've seen in some time."

"Well, he tried to commit suicide or something in Tim's apartment last night."

It was strange having that two-by-four cheese box at the Casbah referred to as an apartment. "Isn't that pathetic! I remember him so well in the silents."

Mr. Frobisher turned to me. "What is she talking about?"

"It's true, only the police don't think it was attempted suicide."

"Oh?"

"They think it was just an accident."

"Oh, darling, you didn't tell me you have had the police in and everything." I thought Miss Randall's excitement at that idea was a little ghoulish. "Did they give you a third degree?"

"No. Just asked the usual questions. He's at St. Vincent's. I'm going down at noon to see how he is."

Maggie, who hadn't opened her mouth all during my monologue about Kendall, said slowly, "I can't quite see what he would be doing in your room with a bottle of Lysol in the first place."

"That's what I told the police."

"You must remember he was very drunk at the funeral," said Mr. Frobisher. "He was undoubtedly still drunk and didn't know what he was doing."

Greg, the stage manager, handed Mr. Frobisher his script and he became very businesslike. "I'm sorry, children, but we've got work to do.... Not even a week before Wilmington, and that third act needs a great deal of polishing. Shall we get started? And, Tim, when you see Thayer, find out if there is anything I can do." We took our places for the opening of the third act. "Ready?"

"Curtain," said Greg.

We all knew our lines in the last act now and it was just a question of smoothing-out-business and pointing up. Maggie and I had nothing to do with the plot, and if I had been rewriting this show I would have cut us out quicker than a wink. I had told this to Maggie and she said for me to keep my mouth shut and not go around putting peas in people's ears, whatever that meant. As far as I could see, I simply mixed and poured cocktails and laughed a lot. Maggie, who was supposed to be my wife, had just come down to the country house, which explains why I was in a dinner jacket and she was in an afternoon dress.

Frobisher had suggested movements a couple of times and the author had changed a word here or there but, aside from that, I was on my own. The same with Maggie. I was worried about it at first because our five days weren't up. But Maggie said not to worry, that she'd been asking around and, with Frobisher, it seemed that it was a good sign.

The author, who usually is hell on wheels, was an exception to the rule. He was a big radio writer and this show was just a luxury to him...time off from the soap

operas. He didn't spend much time in the theater, being
vital at the radio studios to see that the housewives got
their vicarious thrills in evenly mounting doses. I meant
to get to work on him and maybe he could fix it so I could
get a couple of shots in his radio stuff, but he wasn't
around very much and didn't seem particularly interested
in me when he was. What progress there was, Maggie
seemed to be making. He thought she was very funny, and
when she wasn't sitting with me they were giggling off
in a corner. That didn't make me feel any better, either. In
the first place she didn't need the job and in the second
place, why didn't he stick to his radio cuties?

At twelve-thirty we broke for lunch. Maggie insisted
on coming with me to St. Vincent's, which surprised me.

"You'll probably miss your lunch."

"So will you, but we can send out for sandwiches.
Besides, I want to see the poor old thing."

"Why this sudden interest? Thought we were only
supposed to think happy thoughts until after opening
night?"

"Never mind…just say I've always had a yen to do
the *Lady with the Lamp.*"

"Are you sure you don't want to ask our author
along? He might get some peachy material."

"Oh, don't be silly. So that's what's been eating
you recently?"

"Nothing's been eating me recently."

St. Vincent's Hospital was cold and uncomfortable-
looking from the outside. Even the women's jail a couple

of blocks east is much fancier. A few nurses and doctors
were just coming back from coffee at the corner drugstore when we arrived. We went in and I explained to the
middle-aged woman at the reception desk what I wanted.

"Is Mr. Thayer a relative of yours?" she asked
sharply. "Visiting hours are from one-thirty to two-thirty
only." I told her he wasn't a relative but a friend, and if
I couldn't see Mr. Thayer could I see the doctor that
attended him? I didn't have much time. She looked
through some card index and made a phone call and told
us to wait in the reception room and she would see what
she could do. We went in and sat down. There were a
few other people in there with us, and Maggie and I
spent ten minutes speculating in hushed tones just which
of the men were expectant fathers and which of the
women were expectant mothers. We decided all the men
looked expectant and none of the women. Presently the
woman that had been behind the desk appeared in the
door with a doctor and pointed us out to him. He came
over and shook hands. He was thin in his shortsleeved
white jacket and very nervous, which you don't expect
to find in doctors—that's the patients' characteristic.
The cloud of disinfectant that radiated from him reminded me of last night, and I could feel my stomach
winding up. We told him what we were there for and he
led us to a bare little room just behind the reception
desk.

"Are you Mr. Briscoe, Mr. Timothy Briscoe?" he
asked. His voice was dry and quick. He probably hadn't
had enough sleep. "The patient was asking for you."

"How is he?"

"Oh, he died this morning." He needn't have been quite so offhand about it as though he were trying to show how tough he was. I don't know what else he could have said, but it was his tone I objected to.

"But how?" I couldn't believe it. "What from?"

"Acute alcoholism mostly. And then the shock helped."

"But it doesn't seem possible." I put my arm around Maggie.

"Best thing, really. He was blinded, you know... that acid."

"Was he conscious at all?"

"Oh, yes, for a little. That's how I remember your name."

"Well, why didn't you notify me? I could have been over here in ten minutes."

"In the first place—" he acted as though I was a child of three and not right bright at that "—he didn't think to give us your phone number and, in the second place, we don't happen to have enough nurses and doctors around this place to go ringing doorbells." I wanted to pop him. Maggie put her hand on my arm.

"Did he say anything else, Doctor, aside from asking for Mr. Briscoe?"

"He may have, miss." He didn't take the same tone with Maggie as he did with me. "We were pretty rushed last night in Emergency. He was only conscious for a few minutes, and we had to dope him up again. He was in pretty bad pain."

"Where is he now? Could we see him?" I was surprised at all this sudden interest on Maggie's part.

"No, they came and got him this morning. At least I think they did. You can check with the girl at the desk. I'm sorry but I've got to go now. It wasn't so bad…he didn't know what had happened. I'm surprised he lived as long as he did." He hurried away.

We asked at the desk and, after several more phone calls, the woman wrote down the name of an undertaker in Maplewood, N. J., and also the name of a brother I didn't even know Kendall had, who lived there. We thanked the woman at the desk and left the hospital.

"Well, that's that," I said.

"Timmy, what did you do with the Youth and Beauty Book? Did you burn it?"

"No, it's back at the Casbah," I said. I was puzzled by her question. "Why?"

"Oh, nothing." We walked on a little way. "Are you sure?" she said suddenly.

"Of course I'm sure. Why wouldn't it be?"

"I was just wondering. When did you see it last?"

"Why, let me see." I thought back. The last time I had actually seen it was when I put it in my breast pocket at her apartment. I told her that. "That was the last time I actually saw it. It must still be in my suit in the closet. What are you getting at? Now don't tell me you're getting the bug! Do you really think this has some connection with Nellie?" I honestly hadn't thought of any connection up until now, which was funny, because before I had thought everything was suspicious.

"What time is it?" It was almost one. "How long would it take to get to your place?"

"The Casbah? Just a couple of minutes' walk. Why?"

"I'd like to see if the book is still there. We've got time. It won't matter if we're a few minutes late. They know we went down to the hospital, or at least that you did." We didn't say anything while we walked the last two blocks to the Casbah. There didn't seem to be anything much to say and we needed our breath, for by the time we got there we were almost running. We pounded up the stairs. I was a little ahead of Maggie. My room still had that smell in it even though Helga had cleaned it thoroughly and had left the window open. I threw open the door of my closet and grabbed the gray suit. Maggie had come in by that time and she watched me as I tried the breast pocket first, then all the other pockets. But, of course, the Youth and Beauty Book was gone.

# CHAPTER SIXTEEN

WE STOOD LOOKING AT each other, my coat dragging on the floor.

"I don't suppose it could be anyplace else, could it?" she said hopefully.

"No." I sat down on the bed and Maggie came and sat beside me. "I haven't worn this suit since then." I got up and looked in the bottom of the closet but I knew it wasn't any use. The book was gone.

"Well," said Maggie. "I'm on your side now. Where do I sign up?"

"What made you change all of a sudden? After all that pep talk about me ending up in Bellevue, this seems to me very sudden."

"It's that Lysol. I wish I could have seen him, but if it was like you told me, it only means one thing."

"What's that?"

"That someone deliberately poured that acid in his face. They meant to blind him."

"Oh God, I can't believe that! The cop assumed it was an accident without any question."

"Have you ever taken a good look at a Lysol bottle?"

"Last night when I was trying to find out what you do."

"Well, it doesn't have a very wide mouth, does it?"

"No. So what?"

"So just dropping it, if you fell down, wouldn't make it pour all over your face, especially your eyes. That's where you said it was mostly, didn't you?"

"Maybe he knew something."

"Why didn't they kill him and be done with it? Oh, darling, I'm scared." She put her head on my shoulder and, to my amazement, started to cry. That wasn't like her. I don't remember her ever having cried before...not really. Not the way she was crying now with deep shaking sobs. I lifted up her head. She pulled the handkerchief out of my pocket and started dabbing at her eyes.

"Hey, wait a minute. Don't go all weepy on me. What's the matter?"

She blew her nose and stuffed my handkerchief in her purse.

"Don't you see, you damn fool? This is your room."

"A poor thing but mine own. What of it?"

"Maybe that acid wasn't meant for that old man at all. Maybe whoever did it thought he was pouring it on your eyes." She started crying again. My stomach, which was just quieting down after the last whiff of Lysol, went into action again. It had never occurred to me that I might have been clawing at my white eyes on this same bed; I clamped my eyes shut and put my hands over them. I could almost feel them burning. In a moment I realized how silly I was being. Maggie finished snuffling and started fixing her face in the mirror over the dresser.

"We'd better get on back to rehearsal. It's after one." I suddenly wanted to get out of this room very badly. "Ready?"

"Is there anything else missing?" I hurriedly looked in the closet, through the dresser drawers and on the table by the bed. Those and a couple of chairs were my furniture.

"No, I don't think so. At least I can't think of anything now. I didn't have time to go through old letters, but there couldn't be anything in them that anyone would want."

"No compromising ones?" Maggie tried to smile. Under the circumstances, it was a pretty good attempt.

"Not a one. Only…"

"Only what?"

"Nothing. Come on, let's go." Something was hanging around in the back of my mind waiting to be thought of, but it wouldn't come and we were already late for rehearsal. In the cab, going up, neither of us said anything until around Herald Square. I had been trying to think of what it was that kept scratching in the back of my brain, and Maggie had been thinking, too, and had come to a conclusion.

"Timmy, you're going to the police. Right after rehearsal. You're going to see somebody and tell them the whole thing. It's silly going on like this and we're not going to take any more chances." I'd thought of that, too.

"But what'll I tell them? That we don't think Nellie died of heart failure? You do agree with me there, don't you?"

"I'm not so sure about that, but I do think there is something definitely off-color about this last little episode."

"But the police were the ones that said it was an accident."

"That was just the cop on the beat. They're not supposed to know anything about things like that. They are just supposed to take in drunks and steal apples...and rattle doorknobs. But we can look up the nearest precinct in the phone book and go see whoever is in charge."

"Oh, now you're going with me? Well, at least that's some comfort, but I still don't know what I'll tell them or what you can expect them to do. They can't dig up Nellie."

"Never mind about Nellie. They must have pulled her apart when they had her and if there had been anything strange there, we would have heard about it. But this other thing—you've got something to go on. There must be fingerprints and things like that. They'll know what to do."

"I took care of all the fingerprints, I'm afraid. I don't even know where that bottle is now, unless Helga has it, and I wiped the top of my dresser off myself. There was blood on it."

"Well, how did they get into your room, then? Or how did Kendall get in, for that matter?"

"The cop was of the opinion that I didn't lock my door, or that Helga left it open when she cleaned it...." All at once an idea hit me. "Jan," I said.

"Who's Jan?"

"Helga's little boy. He has some pixie friends. He knows where she keeps another pass key. Maybe he let Kendall in. He did me the other night when I'd given my key to Kendall and he forgot to give it back. I'll see him tonight."

"Take him over to the station with you."

"I'm not sure that a four-year-old child is the best witness, but you're right. I will. Right after rehearsal." We pulled up in front of the stage door. There were some stagehands standing outside it on the sidewalk, and when we went in we realized that it was Saturday and the show playing there had a matinee. The doorman told us that Mr. Frobisher had left word that the afternoon rehearsal would be at his apartment in case he had neglected to inform the cast, which he had us.

We got another cab and beat it over to Sutton Place. With all this rushing about, Maggie was going to have spent all her first week's salary on cabs alone.

## CHAPTER SEVENTEEN

As WE WERE TAKING THE ELEVATOR up to the apartment, Maggie said that maybe it would be better if we didn't mention all this business to the rest of the company.

"There's no point in getting them all excited. You know how actors are. They'll want to make a big thing of it and then, if we're wrong, we'll feel pretty stupid."

When we got there the butler opened the door and it didn't matter that we were late. They were still on the second act. Frobisher looked up and nodded to us and motioned us to chairs at one end of the room. We sat down and watched the rehearsal.

Frobisher gave them a ten-minute break before starting the third act and everyone came over to us and wanted to know how Kendall was. When we told them he was dead, they were all duly sympathetic.

"It's probably just as well," said Miss Randall very practically. "The pain would have been awful."

"Has somebody made arrangements for burial?" said Mr. Frobisher. "I don't imagine he had any money." I told them that there was a brother who had taken care of all that already. "Why ever do you suppose he did it?

Did he leave a note?" Maggie and I looked at each other. We hadn't thought of that. I'd look through his room as soon as I got back unless Helga had beaten me to it.

"No, I don't believe he did. It was just an accident. They said at the hospital that it was acute alcoholism as well as shock that did it. He didn't have too long to live anyway."

"It's really awful, you know." Paul Showers was looking a little pensive. "You've no idea how famous he was. They still mention him at the studio. Pictures must have been a lot more fun in those days if you were on top. Now it's like a factory. Theater, too, for that matter. Look at this show. Does Louise here demand a string quartet?"

"Maybe it would help my performance if I did. How about it, Frobie? Would you give it to me?" She laughed at him. He smiled and shook his head.

"And look at her clothes." Paul was warming up to his subject. "A sweater and skirt with a bandanna tied around her head." Miss Randall certainly didn't look glamorous when she rehearsed. Her nearsighted eyes required thick glasses for reading, which didn't add anything. "Can you see Barbara LaMarr showing up on a set dressed like that? I tell you, those were the days!"

Barbara LaMarr! Bobby LeB.! Why hadn't it occurred to me before? Bobby was a nickname for Barbara as well as Robert or even Roberta, for that matter. I was one hell of a detective overlooking a thing like that. All at once I realized that the rest of the cast was staring at me. I must have been looking glassy-eyed while I was thinking about the name.

Paul was saying, "Don't you think so, Tim?"

I snapped out of it. "Don't I think so what?"

"Don't you think television will take the place of movies?" I didn't remember how the conversation got around to television. Still, with actors, sooner or later it does, but it must have been when I was in my little trance. I said I hoped it would, and then there'd be more work for everybody than there was now when you could—and they almost did—do every radio show on the air with the same three actors. The break was over, and we started the third act. It wasn't until after we had been through my scene twice that they decided to keep on with the act and I got Maggie out on the terrace and told her about the possibility of Bobby LeB. being a girl.

"I don't see how you can tell the police much about that part of it, do you?" Maggie said. "It would be a fine thing if you said, 'I think Nellie was killed by someone named Bobby LeB. Of course, she may be a man or he may be a woman but why don't you arrest her if you can find out who he is.' No, if I were you I'd just stick to Kendall."

"Do you think I ought to mention Nellie's book, then? If I haven't got it, it would seem pretty feeble asking them to believe that."

"I think you'll do better if you just pretend that Nellie died the way they say.... It's the acid-throwing that I'm worried about, and the sooner you get that straightened out the better I'll feel."

"But suppose they don't pay any attention and just think I'm making up the whole thing? What then?"

"We'll worry about that when the time comes."

We might just as well have started worrying about it then because they didn't believe one word I told them.

## CHAPTER EIGHTEEN

LIEUTENANT HEFFRAN OF the 16th Precinct was very kind and oh, so patient, but it was easy to see that he wished we would stop bothering him with such nonsense and permit him to get back to the more important work of broken store windows and overparked cars. He was heavy and middle-aged and had a face more like an automobile salesman than a detective. He kept rustling papers on his desk in the small bleak office the whole time I was talking to him and, occasionally, made notes on the margins. When he did look up at me during my spiel, his blue eyes were empty. There were no cigars—evidently he didn't smoke—no derby hats…and no attention. I finally got through and he sighed and pushed aside his papers and laid his pencil very deliberately on the desk exactly parallel to the sides. He gave it several little pushes to make sure that it was perfectly aligned before he spoke.

"But, Mr. Briscoe, I don't understand exactly what it is you want me to do."

"I want you to find out who poured that acid in Mr. Thayer's face. That's all."

"According to Johnstone's report, and he's always been a very reliable man, it was simply an accident. These things happen all the time."

"But they don't happen all the time in my room." I was getting mad again. I'd had to work myself up with a good deal of prodding from Maggie to get up nerve enough to go to the police in the first place. I'd never had anything to do with them before and I hadn't wanted to this time, but when Maggie pointed out that perhaps that acid treatment had been meant for me, it put quite a different light on the situation.

Lieutenant Heffran looked at a piece of paper again. It was, I suppose, Johnstone's report.

"It says that there is a possibility that the maid might have left the door open or you might have forgotten to lock it."

"But I tell you that's impossible. I know it was locked and no one else could have gotten in, except..." I thought of Jan. I had meant to stop by and ask him, but Maggie wouldn't let me delay that long. She said that if I put it off one minute, I'd never go to the police at all.

"Except what, Mr. Briscoe?" I had to tell him about Jan having let me in once before. "There you are, you see?" He positively beamed. "In rooming houses like that, almost anyone could have a key. Half the time the same key will open all the doors."

Maggie spoke for the first time. "Then you mean, Lieutenant Heffran, that you refuse to do anything about it?"

"I don't mean anything of the sort, dear lady," he said with a sigh. "I simply don't understand what it is that you want me to do."

"There must be fingerprints—things like that."

"I'm afraid you overestimate the value of fingerprints in a case like this. Mr. Briscoe has told me himself that there were a great many people in the room and that it had been thoroughly cleaned." I didn't remember telling him anything of the sort, but I must have. Anyway there wasn't any use making an issue out of it because it was true. "Johnstone has already been back there today to make a routine check-up and there seemed to be no indication that he should change his original report. If there were one single thing that might suggest that it could have been anything more than a simple accident, I would be glad to do anything I could. You keep saying that the acid was poured on his face deliberately, but at the same time you can't give me any reason for it because he was just a harmless old man, even though Johnstone in his report says that witnesses say he was a confirmed drunk. Johnstone's theory is that Thayer tried to drink the acid and when he got some in his mouth and it started to burn, he jerked or fell back, hit his head on the dresser or whatever it was and fell down and the rest of the acid spilled on his face." And the way he said it, it sounded logical. Only, I knew it wasn't. "You have told me that he has been in your room before—several times, in fact—to use your telephone." I guess I must have given him a very complete history, though I didn't remember it clearly. "If you can tell me one other fact that might suggest some other solution, that's different. As it stands now there is nothing I can do."

"But something was taken from Mr. Briscoe's room. A book," Maggie said. I hadn't mentioned the Youth and Beauty Book. We had agreed not to. But now I was glad she had. It might make him see.

"A book? What kind of a book? Valuable?"

"No," I said. "Not exactly valuable. Just a notebook. It was in my suit pocket hanging in the closet."

"Well, what was in it? Anything of importance?"

"No. Just addresses of actors and producers." To launch into our vague theories about Nellie against this wall of disinterest just didn't seem worthwhile. He wouldn't believe them, anyway.

"You're an actor, then, Mr. Briscoe?" He said the word like it was spelled "l-e-p-e-r." I admitted I was. He looked at Maggie. "Are you in the theater, too?" Maggie said she was and even told him that we were rehearsing in a play at the moment. It was as if an asbestos fire curtain came down behind his eyes. To pin us down with the word *actor* seemed to satisfy him. "I see," he said, and started gathering up the papers on his desk. "Well, I'm afraid that's all I can do for you. If I were you, I'd ask the little boy with the key. Perhaps he has your book. Children often steal things and hide them...or perhaps you mislaid it. It might be a good idea to look over your room again. I'm afraid there's nothing more that I can do for you. Good day." It was as if he had said,

"Go roll your hoop somewhere else, Daddy's busy." And we were out in the hall.

I don't know exactly what I expected the police to do. If I had been able to look at it from Lieutenant Heffran's point of view—which I couldn't because I was so angry—I might have understood his position a little better. But when, as a last resort, you go to the police, you want the same sort of miracle that used to happen when you went to your mother with a skinned knee. Though Lieutenant Heffran was scarcely the type who could kiss it and make it well. I'd keyed myself up to expecting everything and had received—absolutely nothing.

Well, from here on in I was on my own.

Three quick old-fashioneds in the Jumble Shop made us both feel considerably better.

"I still think we should have told him about Nellie," I said.

"It's a good thing you didn't or you'd have been whisked off to Bellevue before you could say 'knife.'" Maggie munched on a pineapple slice. "Did you notice the way he froze up when he found out we were in the theater? You don't suppose he thought we were just trying to get publicity like having a fake jewel robbery?"

"There seems to be only one thing to do," I said.

"Yes. Throw rocks at Lieutenant Heffran. I'm all for it."

"I don't mean that."

"Oh—no, you don't," said Maggie. "That's definitely out, do you hear?"

"I don't know what you're talking about."

"Don't try and pretend. You're planning to keep right on snooping until you end up pushing up daisies like the other two. I know that look in your eye. You've done all you can. You've told the police. If they don't choose to do anything about it, why, that's just too bad."

"But someone has to do something about it. I know now I should have told him about Nellie. Without that, you can't blame him for treating us the way he did. Don't you see, Maggie, you just can't let people get killed and let it go at that. Kendall was a friend of mine."

"That's not true. He was just an old lush that happened to live in the same house, and that's no reason now, just because he's dead, to make out like you were blood brothers and go about avenging him. Besides, what can you do?"

"I can find Bobby LeB. for one thing."

"And then what? Will you just go up to him and say, 'Pardon me, did you kill old Kendall Thayer by chance?' Whoever it is has got that damn book now, which you should never have taken in the first place. That must have been what he wanted, so let it go at that."

"But I don't see what was in that book that was so important. Even if Bobby LeB. did it, the book doesn't prove he was there at the time. I can't see that it proves anything. If he was afraid of it, why didn't he take it when he could have so easily, instead of waiting till now?" I thought this over a minute. "Unless he was in too much of a rush and forgot about it then."

"Tim." Maggie put her finger on my lips to stop my talking. "Tim, let's go to Mexico." This startled me.

"Mexico? What for?"

"Right away. We can fly down tonight maybe or start out on a train. Let's go to Mexico."

"You're nuts. I can't go to Mexico or anyplace else and neither can you. We happen to be in a show, in case you have forgotten."

"We can leave. The five days aren't up. Anybody could do those parts. It wouldn't make the slightest bit of difference. Please, let's go to Mexico."

"Why, you're being ridiculous."

"Never mind about the money. I'll take you."

"Now, wait a minute."

"You'll love it. We can stay in Mexico City for a while, then on to Cuernavaca and Taxco and Acapulco. You'll look divine in one of those Acapulco diapers. And we can watch the boy dive off the rock at La Quebrada, and you can fish if you like, though I personally don't care for it, and we can go to Caleta in the morning and Nornos in the afternoon. And get the most terrific tans. They have fresh coconut oil that you slather all over yourself, and you come out the most heavenly tobacco color in no time at all." There was an urgent tone to her voice that puzzled me. She wasn't drunk, at least not that drunk.

"I do believe you're serious."

"Of course I'm serious. And if you're thinking about

the money, don't give it another thought. It's just ill-gotten gains. I didn't earn it. It was just given to me. David has far more than is good for him, and it's just some more he can take off his income tax, and, anyway, it wouldn't be so much, and if we get tired of Acapulco, we can hire a car and drive all over…maybe down south and see ruins or whatever it is you see down there. What do you say?"

"No," I said. "Thank you very much I'm sure, but no. What's gotten into you all of a sudden?"

"Then you won't go?"

"I can't. You know that. This is the first decent job either of us has had for months and, although I know the parts aren't much, it's in a first-rate production and you know it'll run and it's always easier to get a job when you already have one. Why do you want to leave it now? Tell me what it is that's eating you." All the excitement she had had in her face when she was doing her travelogue faded and she looked old. Little lines that you generally don't notice, pinched in the corners of her eyes. Her voice was flat.

"It's just that if you stay around here you'll keep on snooping, and if you keep on snooping, you'll find out something that somebody doesn't want you to find out, and you'll get acid thrown in your face. I'm just scared. I've got a feeling that everything will be awful if you stick around town, and I don't want people throwing acid in your eyes. I like your eyes. I like them brown, not white. And it won't do any good your saying that you won't keep on snooping, because you will, won't you?"

"Yes."

She just stared at me for a minute, then sighed.

"I thought so. Well, don't say I didn't warn you. Come on, let's get it over with. Where do we start? Where you snoop, there snoop I." She took a mirror out of her purse and examined her face. Then dabbed at it with some powder and lipstick. "God, I look like an old bat! No wonder you jilted my dishonorable proposition. I'll have to go to Lizzie's Monday and get another recap job."

I paid the check and we went out to the street. "What's the first step?" Maggie asked.

"The first step is to get you a cab and send you on home. If I am so damned doomed, I'm not going to have you messing about getting splashed, too."

"Oh, so now it's chivalry? Listen, dear, we're in this thing together. Don't forget my name was in that book, too. I've got just as big a check after my name on somebody's list as you have. Lead on—where first?"

"Well, we've got to be back at rehearsal in an hour. I suppose we ought to eat…we never seem to get around to it these days. But the first thing to do is see if Jan handed out that key to anyone. I can't wait for you to meet Jan's little playmate, Nana. A charming girl six inches high and quite invisible. But just pretend you don't notice she's invisible, because Jan's liable to be sensitive about it."

# CHAPTER NINETEEN

WHEN WE REACHED THE CASBAH there was a 1934 Chevrolet with a New Jersey license plate parked out in front. Jan wasn't in his usual place on the stairs, and Helga wasn't in her room. And I didn't have any messages in my box.

"You might as well wait in my room while I go flush Helga out," I told Maggie. "She's around somewhere."

We walked up the stairs to the third floor. The door to Kendall's room was open and as we passed it, I heard voices. I looked in and there was Helga helping a thin, gray little man stuff Kendall's belongings into his huge wardrobe trunk. Helga asked me to come in and gave Maggie a sharp appraising look as she followed me. There wasn't much room, with the trunk open in the middle of the floor and the breakfast food and soap piled along the walls.

"This here is poor Mr. Thayer's brother come to get his things. This is Mr. Briscoe." I held out my hand, but he ignored it and went on emptying the drawers of the bureau into the trunk.

"I'd like to tell you how sorry I am about you brother, Mr. Thayer."

He paused in his work and looked at me. His face was completely colorless. He still had his hat on but the bits of hair that showed were almost white. It was impossible to believe this drab little man was Kendall's brother. His eyes were expressionless behind glittery gold-rimmed glasses. And when he spoke he scarcely opened his lips. He just squeezed the words through them like toothpaste.

"My name is Slattery and so was his before he changed it." He threw a handful of dirty socks in the trunk drawer, closed it and opened another one. "That name wasn't good enough for him. He had to change it to Kendall Thayer when he got to be an actor. Amos Slattery wasn't good enough for him. Well, it's good enough for him now," he said, viciously stuffing another handful of clothes into the trunk. "That's the name that's going to be on his grave, Amos Slattery. I hope he rests in peace, the son of a bitch."

"You shouldn't say that about your own brother." Helga was horrified. "He was a good man."

"He was a no-good drunken bum. That's what he was. Nothing but trouble since the day he was born. Do you think when he was making all that money in pictures he'd send us any, or even save any? He did not. Spent every damn cent on himself. No insurance. No nothing. Just a lot of crummy clothes and soap and breakfast food and look at these…" And he jerked one of the drawers open so violently that it fell out and scattered newspaper clippings and photographs in a messy heap on the floor. Some of them were yellowed around the edges and crumbled when they hit the floor. "Every one of them telling what a great guy he was. How many bathrooms he had, all about his swimming pool. But who's got to pay for burying him? I have. Who's been keeping him in liquor for the last ten years? I have.... And this is what I get...dirty clothes and newspaper clippings. He should have poured that acid in him long ago instead of spending all my money for whiskey." He jabbed the last of the clothes in the trunk and slammed the drawer. He picked up the drawer that had fallen on the floor and turned it upside down and a few more clippings floated to the floor. Then he grabbed some of the soap cartons and filled the drawer and put it back in the trunk. I helped him close it. "There, I guess that's all." He looked at Helga. "Will you have this expressed to me?" He wrote the address on a piece of paper and handed it to Helga.

"When is the ceremony, Mr. Slattery?" I said. "Kendall was a friend of mine. I'd like to be there."

"There isn't going to be any ceremony."

"What do you want me to do with all this food and soap and these paper clippings?" asked Helga.

"Burn them. Throw them away. I don't care. Send the trunk collect."

Without even nodding goodbye, he rushed out of the room. I could hear him walking down the stairs. None of us said anything till he had made all three flights and we heard the front door slam.

"Whew!" said Maggie. "Nice fellow. So full of brotherly love."

"He shouldn't talk that way about his own brother,"

said Helga, shaking her head. "No one should say that about his own brother.... It's not nice."

Maggie had picked up some of the spilled clippings and was looking through them.

"That policeman come back this morning asking questions," reported Helga. "He called him a bum, too. It's not nice to talk that way about people, even if they are dead."

"What sort of questions, Helga?" I asked.

"If anyone heard anything strange."

"And did they?"

"No. Nothing. But it's not nice to say things like that. He was a good man, Mr. Thayer, even if he did drink. He was a nice man...no bum like they say."

"I know it, Helga."

"Tim, look at this." Maggie handed me a picture cut from *Photoplay*. It was Kendall standing in front of a huge Spanish house. He was in a white shirt opened at the neck and white flannel trousers. Even in the direct sunlight you could see how handsome he was. It was a shock when I remembered the Kendall I was used to—the cigarette bummer...the two-buck borrower—it didn't seem possible that he had ever looked like that and lived in so fancy a house. She shuffled some more of them. Reviews of pictures and plays. All mention of him was carefully underlined in red pencil. All at once, that thought that had been waiting round to be thought hit me. Those clippings that Kendall had brought in for me to read! I hadn't seen them in my room. I hadn't seen them or read them, but they had been on top of my dresser where he had thrown them, and I didn't remember seeing them there.

Helga was starting to clean up the mess, and Maggie was still thumbing through the clippings. I ran back to my room, unlocked the door and looked on the dresser. The clippings were gone. I searched through all the drawers and even the wastebasket, but there was no trace of them. I went back to Kendall's room.

"Helga, did you see some of those clippings on my dresser yesterday?"

"Ja. Just like these."

"What did you do with them?"

"I didn't do nothing with them. I leave them there. I don't take things out of rooms. You know that, Mr. Briscoe."

"Well, maybe Jan did. Where is he, anyway?"

"Oh, no, Mr. Briscoe. Jan wouldn't do a thing like that."

"Well, he knows where you keep your pass key. He got it for me the other night."

"Oh, no. That isn't possible."

"Where do you keep the pass key?"

"On the shelf in the broom closet, but he doesn't know. He's too little to understand."

"Well, where is he? I'd like to ask him about the other night."

"I'll call him, but I know he won't know nothing and he wouldn't do a thing like that." She yelled out the door for him and, before the echo had died out in the maze of halls, Jan was standing in the doorway looking at us soberly with those incredible eyes. Before Helga could start in, I asked her to let me talk to him alone. I didn't doubt that he had heard everything we had said, and perhaps he would think his mother would punish him. Maggie and I led him to my room and I closed the door. We sat on the bed and Jan leaned against the dresser. His head just came to the top of it. I took a quarter out of my pocket and held it in my hand so Jan could see it. "Now, Jan, here's a quarter for you if you'll tell me something." He held out his grimy hand. "No, first you must tell me something and then you can have it." He didn't say anything, but just looked at me.

"Did you come into my room yesterday and take something out of it?" He still didn't say anything.

"It's all right if you did, Jan. I'm not angry with you. I just want you to tell me if you did."

"No," he said. "Gimme money." I handed over the quarter.

"Well, did you open the door for anyone? You remember, like you did for me when I had forgotten my key…you know, with the secret key?" He shook his head violently.

"Won't tell."

"Why not? Surely you can tell me? I'm your friend."

"Promised."

"Promised who, Jan? Who did you promise not to tell?"

"The Phantom."

Maggie and I looked at each other. She shrugged.

"You promised the Phantom you wouldn't tell you opened my door?" He didn't say anything. "Did he give you money, too?"

Jan nodded. I pulled out a fifty-cent piece. This little third degree was getting expensive.

"See this, Jan? I'll give you this if you'll tell. That's more than the Phantom gave you, wasn't it?"

His face lit up at the sight of the money and he reached for it. I held it over his head the way you do a piece of meat for a puppy. "Not until you tell me."

"No," he said stubbornly. And stuck his hands behind his back.

"Nana says it's all right." Maggie brushed me out of the way and knelt down beside him. "I was talking to Nana this morning and she said for me to tell you to tell Mr. Briscoe all about the Phantom." He turned his big eyes on her and opened them even wider.

"She did?" He looked at Maggie as she put her arm around his shoulder. "Honest?"

"Honest," said Maggie. "So you see it's all right. Nana wouldn't tell you it was all right unless it was, would she, Jan?" He thought this over for a minute.

"Last night," he said finally.

"You mean it was last night when the Phantom spoke to you?" He bobbed his head. "What did the Phantom look like? Was it a man like Mr. Briscoe or a girl phantom like me?"

He pointed to me.

"So it was a man phantom? What did he look like, Jan? Did he tell you he was a phantom?"

Jan shook his head. I was getting impatient, but I gritted my teeth and tried to force a lover-of-children smile on my mouth. "Then how did you know he was the Phantom?"

"He had great big green eyes. Great big green eyes like this." And Jan pushed up the corners of his eyes with his two dirty forefingers, the way you indicate Asian eyes.

"Do you mean he was Asian, Jan? You know what an Asian looks like, don't you?"

"He was the Phantom." Then suddenly it clicked. I'd remembered Jan was a comic-book addict and the Phantom in the comic books always had eyes like…exactly like harlequin glasses. I grabbed him by the shoulders and he started to cry. I had to give him the fifty cents before he would shut up and listen to me.

"Had you ever seen him before?" He shook his head. "Did he ask you to open my room specially, or just any room?"

"Your room. Can I go now?"

"Of course you can go. And thank you very much, Jan, and here's another quarter." I gave it to him and he ran out. Maggie and I just remained squatting on the floor for a minute after he left. Finally I helped her up. She sat on the bed and I sat down on one of the two chairs. We both knew what the other was thinking and it wasn't very pleasant.

"That was a neat bit about Nana. Whatever made you think of it?" I didn't want to say what we were thinking. Not just yet.

"Didn't you have imaginary playmates when you were little? Most children do, particularly if they're lonely.… It must be the same man, mustn't it?"

"Yes. Bertha's pal. The one who didn't want to give her his autograph that morning."

"Do you think that's enough proof for Lieutenant Heffran?"

"Just that Bertha didn't get the autograph of a man wearing funny glasses and a little kid, four years old, who says that he opened my door for a phantom? I can hear him laughing now."

"You won't consider Mexico? The offer still goes."

"Thanks, darling, but no."

"I didn't think you would. I don't suppose there's much doubt in your mind, either, that the gent in the funny glasses is Bobby LeB., is there?"

"Is there in yours?"

"Not very much, I'm afraid. So it looks as though you'll never be happy until you find him and get your acid ration. I still don't see why he had to kill poor old Kendall just to get that book."

"Unless he meant to kill me." That was a pleasant thought I always came back to and quickly tried to run away from. "But he didn't mean to kill him. Kendall must have recognized him. But even so, what difference would that make?"

"How did Kendall get mixed up with him, anyway?"

"Maybe he heard Bobby and thought it was me...."

"I."

"Okay. Then came in to see me. He'd left me a note saying that he wanted to see me as soon as I got in."

"But why take the clippings, too? That seems very silly. If you want to take the trouble you can get notices of any show at the library."

"I can't understand that part of it, either. There must

have been something in them. We'll have to do that. Go to the library and find them. We can do that tomorrow."

It took us thirty-five minutes to get to Sutton Place. The Saturday-night traffic didn't seem to care about our rehearsal. Frobisher gave us a very annoyed look as we crept in and sat down in a corner. They had come to the third act and because we weren't there, had skipped the beginning of it and gone on with the rest. He was very highty-tighty as he stopped the rehearsal and said they would take the act from the beginning. I apologized as best I could and told him about the traffic and he thawed out a little and finally, when the rehearsal ended at eleven, he was quite friendly again. Although it was going to take some time for Greg, the stage manager, to forgive me. They take those things very seriously. I wasn't taking it any too lightly, either, because our five days weren't up yet and we could be fired without a cent if Frobisher felt like it.

When we were leaving, I managed to be the last one out. Mr. Frobisher had come to the door to say goodbye. I wasn't sure how he was going to feel about his less glamorous past being mentioned in front of the rest of the cast so had waited till I was more or less alone with him.

"Mr. Frobisher, you were stage manager for one of the shows Thayer was in, weren't you?" He looked at me quizzically.

"So you've found out my humble beginnings? Yes, I was. *Front Page Stuff,* as a matter of fact. Why?"

"Did you ever know anybody connected with that show with a name like Bobby LeB.?" He thought a moment…his forehead wrinkled. "No, I'm sorry, but I don't. It was a long time ago, you must remember, and there are a lot of people in musicals. Stage hands, musicians…there might well have been a Bobby LeB., but I'm afraid I don't remember offhand. Why? Is it very important? Was he a friend of yours?"

"Not exactly. I have a message for him, and, unfortunately, that's all the name I know. You wouldn't have any idea how I could find him, would you?"

"No, I'm afraid not. So much happens to the people in a show in twelve or thirteen years. They give up the profession, the war…all sorts of things. I'm sorry I can't be more helpful."

We said good-night.

Rehearsal wasn't till one o'clock on Sunday so Maggie and I decided to have a nightcap or two before going home. We dropped in at "21" first, since we both now had jobs, and had a drink at the bar. The place was crowded and, as usual, it depressed me. Everyone seemed so damned successful. You could practically see the money ooze.

Old light-of-my-life Ted Kent was there, to add to my depression, with Margo. She must have more money than I had thought. Otherwise I knew Ted wouldn't be sniffing around—plus that mink coat she had thrown around her tonight looked just as expensive as Maggie's, a fact of which I am quite sure Maggie was not unconscious. Ted got Lord of the Manor and called us over to his table, and for once I was almost glad to see him. I had a job and he didn't. Maybe it wasn't so much of a job but in the theater a job is a job is a job is a job. There was, of course, the pause while Ted kissed and *darlinged* Maggie and I gritted my teeth and, out of spite, I almost had a go at Margo but couldn't quite bring myself to it, though I must say she seemed all primed.

We all sat down and Ted couldn't wait for the drinks to finish being ordered before he launched into the newest juicy morsel of gossip he'd unearthed.

"Darlings, have you heard about Harry Bruno…you know the one that owns that dreadful theater on Seventh Avenue." This little darling hadn't heard but this little darling knew that theater quite well having served a very short time in two flops there. "Well, you know he simply can't afford to have a hit in that house, he owes so much money and he makes more out of flops. Believe me, he even goes to the out-of-town openings just to make sure they're bad enough…. Of course, with the theater shortage he can get away with it."

"But, Ted, I don't understand," said Margo. "What do you mean he can't afford to have a hit?" Yes, she was doing all right…she'd learned how to set up Ted. Yes, it wouldn't be long before Ted would be sending out little notes to the columnists saying, "Well-known stage and screen star Ted Kent is blazing with what recently renovated eyeful?" and signing someone else's name. He's done it before and he can do it again. "I should think every theater owner would want a hit." Lay it out for him sister. Give him the topper.

"But don't you see, darling. Every show has to pay for the theater two weeks in advance and if it's a flop and doesn't run two weeks then Harry can keep the money and get another show in right away and that show has to pay two weeks in advance, too."

"Why, I think that's awful," said Margo. "Don't you, Tim?" But Ted wasn't going to let me get into his act.

"Well, anyway, Ed Dell—you know, the critic— hates Harry's guts and thought he'd fix him but good. He knew Harry needed twelve thousand bucks right away or he'd lose the theater, and the only way he could get that much money in the time he had was to have three quick flops. Well, he got two all right and the third one was a stinker, too, but Ed gave it a rave notice in his paper, thinking that would make it run long enough to put Harry out of business—and it would have, too. Only guess what Harry did?"

"What, Ted?" said Margo breathlessly. "I can't imagine." Here was my chance.

"So Harry took the rave notice," I said before Ted could stop me. "And went to a loan shark and borrowed the twelve thousand dollars on the strength of Ed's rave notices and lived happily ever after." Ted, I am glad to say, was livid.

"I think after that, Tim," said Maggie, "the least we can do is leave." She got up and I helped her on with her coat.

"Libby told me about their offering you that part in the Equity Library show, Margo," I said. Ted was still sulking. "I think you'd have gotten more experience from that than understudying."

"Oh, that was just Libby's idea, and even if I did want to act I'm certainly not ready for Ibsen yet. Can you imagine me as Nora in *A Doll's House?*"

"Libby said it was Rosalind in *As You Like It*. I should think you'd be a good type for that."

"Oh, you know Libby, how vague she is. It was *A Doll's House* and I'm certainly not up to that."

"How's your walk-on in the new Frobisher thing?" said Ted. That was a feeble effort to get back at me. He knew it was more than a walk-on.

"It's shaping up." He wasn't going to get any change out of me.

"When do you open?"

"Wilmington, Friday."

"I might run up and catch it if I can. I've always liked Randall's work, but I'm surprised in her position she couldn't make Frobie get someone better to play opposite her than Paul Showers." Someone like Ted Kent, no doubt. I knew what the next line would be. It always is. "They offered it to me, but I couldn't let Terry and Lawrence down. What's Showers doing back here, anyway? Didn't they pick up his option?"

"Just slumming like the rest of us."

"Well, good luck. Carry your spear pretty. I'll try and remember, but if I forget, consider yourself sent a wire opening night."

"Thanks, I'll do that little thing." I bought back my coat and hat from the checkroom and we hit Fifty-second Street, but not soon enough. The fair Diana was just getting out of a taxi. I toyed with the idea of ducking back into the bar but it was too late. She had seen me. The look and nod I got were reserved exclusively for brass monkeys. Well, that's done it. You've had it, chum.

It's going to take a great deal of explaining to get back on her Christmas list. But what do you know? Suddenly I realized I didn't care. To hell with that. I'd jumped through Diana's rather peculiar hoops for the last time.

"What are you laughing about?" asked Maggie while we were waiting for a cab.

"I hadn't realized I was laughing."

"Well, you were. It sounded nice. You should do it more often."

I kissed Maggie and meant it. "Well," said Maggie breathlessly. "You should do *that* more often, too."

# CHAPTER TWENTY

As I STARTED TO CLIMB the Casbah stairs, I remembered that I wanted to ask Helga to let me in Kendall's room to see if he had anything there that might suggest why he got the acid facial—there was just a chance, not much of one, but I didn't want to overlook any bets. I knocked at Helga's door and waited. Nothing happened so this time I pounded. After a moment she asked who was there and I told her and said it was important that I see her. I had to wait a couple of more minutes until she finally unlocked and opened the door just wide enough for her to slip out into the hall and closed it quickly after her. I didn't have to wonder why. She had a silk kimono clutched around her and as far as I could see nothing else.

"What you want, Tim? Come back tomorrow."

"Sorry to bother you, Helga, but it's important. I want to look through Kendall's room."

"It's empty. All cleaned up. Everything." So that was no good.

"But, Helga, didn't you find anything when you were cleaning it up? Something that might give an idea about what he was doing that night. A magazine he was reading…or a paper?"

"Why you want to know?" she asked suspiciously.

"Because I want to find out how he was killed."

"Policeman said it was accident."

"I know he did, but I just want to find out how the accident happened. He was my friend, Helga." She looked at me for a moment then did a quick flick around the door and almost immediately reappeared, still without letting me get a glimpse into her room. She handed me a piece of notepaper with some writing on it.

"This was on the floor. Must have fallen off table. I was going to send it to his brother." I recognized Kendall's florid handwriting. It was the beginning of a letter:

Friday

Dear Bobby,

*"Can such things be and overcome us like a summer's cloud without our special wonder?" My wants are few and it will unquestionably be to your advantage to revive old memories. "Wilt thou at Ninny's tomb meet me straightaway?" Say, three o'clock Monday. I was amused to see—*

—and it stopped there. I tried to keep my voice calm.

"Let me have this for a couple of days, Helga. I'll give it back."

"What you want it for? You won't get me in trouble?"

"No. I promise." Then I thought of something. "Helga, listen, this is important. Was there an envelope with this? Think carefully."

"No, that was all, and I ought to send it to his brother."

"But, Helga, you know as well as I do Kendall's brother doesn't care a damn about him. You heard him."

"He shouldn't have said that about his own brother. He was no bum like he said."

"Of course he wasn't. Thanks, Helga." Before she could say anything else I ran up the stairs.

I went into my room, locked the door and sat down on the bed. Three more readings of the letter didn't tell me anything new, but it was written to Bobby, and in my little world there was only one Bobby I was interested in and I was positive this was written to that one—Bobby LeB. I didn't recognize the quotations, but then I wouldn't. There didn't seem to be much doubt that Ninny's tomb referred to either Nellie's office or the funeral parlor. Maybe Maggie would know. I phoned her and she'd just gotten in. I told her about the letter. For some reason I almost whispered it over the phone.

"Kendall was quite the Shakespearean scholar, wasn't he? Ninny's tomb is from *Midsummer Night's Dream*," she said rather superciliously, I thought. "The Pyramus and Thisbe scene."

"How in the world did you know that?"

"We did it at college and, I might add, I was ravishing as Titania, but I don't know the other quote. What do you suppose it means?"

"I hoped you'd know."

"But are you sure this Bobby is the one we want? There are lots of Bobbys in the world, you know."

"Only one I'm interested in."

"Well, take care of yourself, my darling. Sweet Shakespearean dreams."

"Maggie, have breakfast with me tomorrow morning?"

"But it's Sunday."

"The Brevoort, then. Ten o'clock. That'll give us time to go by the library before rehearsal."

"The library?"

"Don't you remember? To look up the *Front Page Stuff* notices?"

"Oh my God."

"Ten o'clock, Brevoort."

"Okay. Well, good night."

"Good night." I started to hang up.

"Oh, say, Timmy…"

"Yes?"

"If I were you, I'd lock my window and put a chair under my door."

"Don't worry about me." I laughed. "I can take care of myself. Good night."

But, feeling like a damn fool, I did lock my window and I did put the chair under my door.

# CHAPTER TWENTY-ONE

OF COURSE IT NEVER occurred to either of us to telephone first to make sure, so we didn't find out till we got all the way up to the public library that the back newspaper file department is closed on Sunday.

"A pretty how-do-you-do! Now what?" said Maggie. "Go back to the Brevoort and have me watch you stuff yourself some more?"

We were standing in front of the information desk feeling a little letdown. But people seemed to be taking books out under their arms—those departments were still functioning on Sunday—and there were books that had, at least, the casts of all the plays, if not the reviews. That might help some. Like those Burns Mantle *Best Plays of* things. Maggie had mentioned them only the other night. Maggie sighed and obediently followed me up to those caverns where you get books. After duly looking it up on index cards and filling out the little slip, we waited in another enormous room until our number flashed on the indicator and we were presented with *Best Plays of 1934*.

Seeing the titles of the best plays brought 1934

back with a rush. The theater was all very glamorous then. I had seen all the plays listed as best, too. *Dodsworth* and *Ah Wilderness* and *The Shining Hour* and *The Green Bay Tree* and *Mary of Scotland*. I was afraid *A Kiss Thrown In* would seem pretty pallid by comparison.

Sure enough, listed in the back was *Front Page Stuff* with the cast of characters and a brief synopsis. Kendall was there and Nellie and then at the bottom where the "also among those present" were grouped together, one name came whirling up at me. Instead of calling it the chorus, the boys and girls in *Front Page Stuff* were classified "Headliners and Featurettes," pretty fancy, that. There among the names of the six headliners was the baby we'd been looking for. The last five letters of a six-letter word beginning with B. Robert LeBranch. I felt the library light up like a pinball machine.

"Now, at least we know his name," I whispered to Maggie. "All we've got to do is find him. Chorus Equity'll be sure to know. Have you got a pencil?"

"What for?"

"I want to copy down the rest of the cast."

"Don't be silly. I'm a taxpayer," said Maggie and she took the page and ripped it out of the book. I was aghast. "Come on, we've got to get going. If we're late again we are both definitely out of a job." She handed me the page. I furtively stuck it in my pocket.

"Maggie, you shouldn't do that," I said.

"I always do. You wanted those names, didn't you? Come on." We left—me expecting any minute a guard would tap me on the shoulder and beckon me to follow him to some dim vault in the public library where they do awful things to people who tear pages out of *Best Plays of 1934.* "You can't take books out of the reference room, can you?" she said when we were safely through the turnstiles and out on the steps. I admitted you couldn't. "Well then, we're late now and would be a great deal later if you'd written all that stuff out. Don't make such a thing of it." We beat it for the Lyceum. It didn't seem possible that I could be so shocked. People could kill other people or throw acid in their face, but people didn't tear pages out of library books.

The rehearsal seemed endless. We were having straight run-throughs now, but Greg insisted that we stand by the entire time, which seemed rather pointless to me, but he said those were Mr. Frobisher's orders, so I didn't quite quibble. During the first and second act I went out to the pay telephone in the hall and tried to find some of the *Front Page Stuff* cast in the phone book. A few of the principals were listed but I figured they'd be the least likely to remember a member of a chorus fourteen years ago. The principals speak only to themselves and sometimes not even that. The bit players ignore each other and try to talk to the principals, and no one ever speaks to the chorus except possibly the baritone or the comic who tries to sleep with every one of the chorus girls before the show closes and, more often than not, succeeds—particularly when he can get them fired if they aren't susceptible to his charms. On an off chance, I even called

Chorus Equity, but there was no answer. Only one of the headliners and featurettes was listed, which, considering it was fourteen years ago that the show played, was not too surprising. The single exception was a Peter Peters who had a dance studio on West Twenty-third Street. The life span of a chorus boy or girl is comparatively short. The girls, I suppose, manage to marry someone and can leave off their girdles for good, but I never can figure out what happens to superannuated chorus boys as a rule. Mr. Peters had apparently opened a dance studio. But the rest of them must get into a final Off-To-Buffalo and just keep going, or else get in the road company of the *Student Prince.* I dialed Mr. Peter Peters's number and he miraculously not only answered the phone but was the same one that had been a headliner.

"Yeah," said the soft, rather high voice of Mr. Peters. "I was in that show, so what? You trying to collect dues for something? You're a little late, bud."

"No," I said, "I'm just trying to find someone else who was in it and you're the only one I could find with a phone."

"My God, that was ages ago. Who are you trying to find?"

"A Mr. Robert LeBranch. Do you remember him?"

There was a long pause. Finally… "What do you want him for?"

"I'm from out of town and wanted to look him up."

"Who'd you say this was calling?" I gave him the name of my character in the show, Dan Kelley. "A friend of his, you say?" I repeated that I was.

"Sorry, fella. I don't know. Haven't seen him since the show."

"Well, thanks anyway." I started to hang up.

"Wait a minute. What'd you say your name was?" I told him again. "Kelley, eh? Hoofer?"

"No. Just a friend."

"What are you doing tonight? Why don't you drop around for a drink? I can ask around. Might find out something for you. We could have a couple of laughs—see some sights." My quest for Mr. LeB. seemed to be widening my circle of acquaintances.

"Thanks. I might do that. What time?"

"Anytime. I'll be here. You got the address in the book. I live in the back of the studio. The later the better, it'll give me time to ask around."

"Okay, I'll do that."

"It's a date."

"Yeah. See you later. Goodbye." I hung up the receiver and turned to face Maggie's amused look.

"Get him!" she said. "Got a date with a chorus boy, have you? What are you going to do? Drink champagne out of his slipper?"

"Oh, shut up."

"What did you find out about our mutual friend Mr. LeBranch?"

"He remembers him. Think I'll drop over after rehearsal and see what he knows. I tell you what I wish you'd do for me."

"I think he'd rather you went alone."

"Never mind about him, but tomorrow morning I

wish you'd go to Chorus Equity and find out what you can there."

"I've got a fitting at Ernie's tomorrow morning."

"Well, do it before that. And while you're at Ernie's find out what else you can about that niece of Nellie's. I still can't get over that. Maybe Ernie was lying."

"Okay, boss. If I'm good can I have a drink out of the office bottle like a real private eye?"

"We'd better get back onstage or there won't be any bottle at all. They must be almost through with the second act."

We went back and rehearsed and sat around and ate and went to Frobisher's apartment and sat around and rehearsed and then just sat around.

Just as we were saying good-night, Mr. Frobisher called us over and told us we could forget about the five-day clause. We were in! I could have kissed him, and Maggie did.

Up until that minute I had half expected Greg or Mr. Frobisher to give me the old line about "It has nothing to do with your performance, but the author feels you're just a little too old for the part, I'm sure you'll understand," and then you say that of course you understand perfectly and it's quite all right and thank you so much, and you leave with your eyes tight and your mouth set in a deathlike grin and you get somewhere alone just as fast as you can and get as drunk as you can afford.

But evidently I had become a member of what the ads would call "a distinguished cast" and I was sure of at least two weeks' salary. I had a few bubbles in my shoes and decided to skate on over to Twenty-third Street while I still had them. And to celebrate I stopped for a couple of drinks on the way.

## *CHAPTER TWENTY-TWO*

THE PETERS STUDIO WAS IN a second-floor loft over a store selling dress trimmings. The store windows glittered with sequins even in the feeble light of the streetlamp. In a little entrance at the side of the trimming store was a push button under a card saying "Peters Dancing Studio." I pushed the button and waited.

I felt I knew pretty much what to expect. You don't hang around the theater for over ten years without getting to know the stereotype of the chorus boy. I had imagined from his voice that Peters was going to be that stereotype. But, whatever I was expecting, I was wrong.

Peters opened the door and I thought, at first, I had made a mistake. He was a good-looking, practically blue-shirt lead, curly red hair—almost crew-cut—a good pair of shoulders under an open-collared shirt. No rings. No bracelets. If I hadn't known he had been in a show fourteen years ago I would have guessed his age at about twenty-five. I must do more dancing, maybe I can knock a few years off me. The only thing that gave him away was his voice and his eyes—they were both a little too soft, and he had that trick of widening his blue eyes to punctuate his sentences.

We shook hands and he said that he hadn't expected me to drop in, really, and I said I hadn't expected to, really. I followed him upstairs and through a big empty room with a huge mirror on one wall and a battered piano with a portable victrola on top of it against another. He lived in the rear of the studio and it was fixed up very comfortably. Long monk's-cloth curtains completely covered the high windows and a studio couch had a monk's-cloth slipcover. A folding screen partially hid an icebox, stove and sink kitchenette. Low, modern, paint-it-yourself bookcases were filled with books and records and the white walls were plastered with photographs—mostly of male dancers with a few of the more angular females of the Martha Graham school, as well as scattered wrestlers and prizefighters popping their oiled muscles and puffing out their chests. There were also a couple of production flashes of different shows. I began to get hopeful when I saw those. Maybe Bobby LeB. was one of the toothy gents making that stock pose with the top hat, cane and modernistic background that dancers seem to love so.

Peters was apparently getting more hopeful, too, and had broken out a bottle of good Scotch. He went behind the screen and got ice and soda and came back with a couple of stiff ones. I sat in an armchair and he arranged himself on the studio couch. I noticed that my drink was about twice as dark as his. Evidently he was under the impression that we were in for a nice, long evening.

I asked him about the dancing-school business and he was quite amusing telling me about it. Most of his pupils were children and all doomed to go through life with their mothers convinced that they were better than Shirley Temple and Margaret O'Brien put together. It was, he admitted, quite a racket. You charge them a tidy sum for the lesson and twice a year you'd give a recital and the little kiddies would have to sell so many tickets or they couldn't be in it. Or, if they were, only as background. A specialty in a Peters recital came high in tickets. Besides that, they would have to buy costumes, which was another rake-off for him. All in all, it was a very profitable business, but, of course, not very satisfying to the "inner longing," if I knew what he meant. And I did.

He was about to go more deeply into his inner longings when the phone rang. I studied the pictures on the wall while he answered it. I gathered one of his friends was determined to come up and see Peters, and Peters was just as determined that he shouldn't.

"I tell you I won't have you coming up here." He all but stamped his foot. I caught his eyes and he shrugged resignedly. "Yes…yes…later… No, I tell you it's simply out of the question." And he slammed the receiver back on the cradle. "You'd think people would know when they're not wanted, wouldn't you?" he said. "*Mais non.* Some people never learn." He came back and sat down and I asked him about Bobby.

It turned out that Peters hadn't known him too well. They'd dressed in the same dressing room with the rest of the headliners in *Front Page Stuff,* but he didn't see much of him outside the theater.

"Bobby was more the social type," Peters said with a double-header widening of those blue eyes. "I don't wonder that he gave up the theater, he was a lousy dancer really. How well did you know him?" There was a sidewinding look with that one.

"Oh, I never knew him at all, really. He's just a friend of a friend back home that asked me to look him up."

"And where is back home, Mr. Briscoe?"

"Indiana," I said. I don't know why. "Evansville, Indiana. I've never even seen Bobby, you know, and I'm curious to know what he looks like. Is one of those him?" I nodded to the wall. Peters got up from the couch and took one picture down and handed it to me.

"That's the headliners. Of course, we were just called that in the show. We weren't a standard act." He rested his hand on my shoulder as he sat on the arm of my chair and with his other hand he pointed out the third man from the left. "That's Bobby."

So that was Bobby LeB. His face had about as much expression as one of those animated dolls that hold up placards in cheap store windows. The kind of doll where the eyebrows swivel up and down and the head turns back and forth. The smile was just as frozen and the hair just as painted, black and straight, the face perfectly smooth, eyebrows sharply arched, but, then, the picture had been taken in stage makeup. You could see the black line around the eyes and the carefully bowed mouths. The headliners were all about the same height, all dressed in evening clothes and standing one in front of the other with the left leg pointed forward and the left hand holding the elbow of the man in front. The right hand was waving a top hat. Just the usual corny dancer picture.

I didn't know whether I would be able to tell that face again if I saw it or not. It might have changed a great deal and with all the goo you couldn't tell what the real face looked like, anyway.

"Have you any idea how I could go about finding him?" I asked when I had finished looking at the picture.

"No. I'm sorry but I can't imagine where you could look."

"Evansville is going to be terribly disappointed. Well, thanks for the drink. I've got to be going." I started to get up, but his arm very gently held me back in the chair.

"Going? Going where?"

"I've got to get an early start in the morning back to Evansville." I shook his arm off and got up. He didn't try and stop me this time. I didn't particularly want to get on the muscle about it so I pretended I hadn't noticed. I put on my coat and hat, which I had thrown on a chair when I came in.

"But you can't go now. I mean, I thought we might make the rounds. I know some amusing places. I'm sure you'd like them."

"Some other time," I said. "I'm tired. I had a busy day. Thanks for the drink. Good night."

He didn't bother to see me to the door so I walked through the studio and let myself out and walked down the stairs and on out to Twenty-third Street.

It wasn't till I walked half a block that I realized that I hadn't been so smart after all. I couldn't be sure, but thinking back, I seemed to remember he had called me "Mr. Briscoe" and I had told him my name was

"Kelley." Another thing, the cast in the Burns Mantle collection had listed six names for the headliners and that picture Peters had shown me had eight little smiling faces all in a row.

I couldn't understand why he had bothered to tell me anything in the first place and then asked me up. Why that? If he wanted to lie about it... But there's a lot of things I don't understand, and I gave up Mr. Peters as one of them.

I could see the neon light of an open all-night one-arm joint a block west so I went in and had some fried eggs and coffee. The coffee was bad and the eggs had been around much too long and it made me sick to my stomach. I left in a rush and the fresh air and sudden misty rain felt so good, I decided to walk up to the Twenty-eighth Street subway station. I couldn't face right away that subway smell and those little piles of wet sawdust the cleaning people plant now and dig later.

It says somewhere that there are about eight million people in New York, but you'd never guess it tonight. At two-thirty, Ninth Avenue was as empty as Twenty-third Street had been.

About Twenty-sixth Street, I began to get dizzy and little sparks were swimming around in my eyes. The eggs must have been older than I thought. I stopped walking and, in a little alleyway, leaned up against the side of a building. I pressed my forehead against the stone and the coolness helped for a moment, but then my mouth started filling with saliva and I simply stood there—waiting to be sick.

I didn't hear footsteps behind me. I didn't hear anything. I just leaned against the wall with my neck wide open for a rabbit-punch—and it came.

My forehead ground against the rough stone as I slid down the wall to my knees and keeled over on my back. I choked and vomited. Something kicked me a couple of times in the ribs and I spewed again. I tried to get up, but a hand like a brick slapped against my face and I fell back.

There was water in the alley. I could feel the coldness soaking through my clothes. I lay there gasping for breath. My eyes wouldn't focus; the stringy wetness all but blinded me. I was vaguely conscious of a couple of looming shapes standing over me silhouetted against a patch of glow between building walls. One of the shapes presently kicked me in the groin. Red searing pain exploded in me and I doubled up, grabbing myself. There was a sharp click and in the dimness I thought I could make out the glitter of a knife blade. I went through all the business of yelling but I couldn't be sure any sound came out of my throat at all. One of the shapes had a voice. It said softly, "Hold it, someone's coming." A foot crashed on the backs of my hands and I was out for the count.

## CHAPTER TWENTY-THREE

"LIFE SAVER," A VOICE kept saying. "Life Saver." I tried to open my eyes. The voice kept repeating, "Life Saver." I wiped my eyes.... They felt crusty and when I opened them I still couldn't see anything. Somebody said "Life Saver" again and I realized I was doing it. Flat on my back in a puddle. I groped around with my hand. It got wet cement. I tried to move and pain made me stop. I gritted my teeth and forced myself to roll over and struggle to my knees. Then I tried to stand. I could do it by inching up the building wall, but when I got to my feet the effort made me lean against the building for a minute or two. I was panting and weak, but my legs held. I took a deep breath. It hurt, but not as if there were ribs broken. I felt my body. It was wet and covered with slime, but it would still function. To feel for my hat I had to bend over, and the rush of blood to my neck almost made me keel over. I had to stand up again until the pounding stopped.

"Here's your hat, mister," said a voice and my hat was slapped on the top of my head. Fear washed over me again. I flattened myself against the wall blindly waiting for it to happen. I had thought I was alone—a hit-and-run—but they had come back. I waited for the knife. I was too weak to do anything to stop it. I started to cry.

"Come on," said a man's voice. "He's okay now. We can't stand around here all night."

"But, Joey, he's hurt." It was the same voice that had given me my hat and it was a woman's voice. "We got to take him somewhere."

"He's just a drunk, I tell you. Come on. He'll be all right." The tears must have rinsed out my eyes enough, for, at last, I could see a man and woman backed by the faint light from the street, standing in front of me. He took her arm and tried to lead her back to the sidewalk. She shook it off.

"I'm not going to leave him standing here like this. He's hurt, Joey. He's hurt bad." She moved toward me. I didn't mean to, but unconsciously I scraped along the wall away from her. She stretched out her hand.

"For Christ's sake, don't touch him. He stinks. You'll get it all over you."

"Go on if you want to, you jerk, he's hurt. I'm not going to leave him here like this." She stepped closer to me. I didn't back away this time. "What happened to you, mister? Were they trying to roll you? We heard them running up the alley." I managed a feeble croak. "Know who they were?"

"No. I couldn't see them." Still bracing myself against the building, I patted my pocket. My billfold was still there. My watch was still on my wrist. I began to be conscious of the cold. I was soaked through and my teeth started to chatter.

"You coming or aren't you?" said the man. She ignored him.

"Can you walk?" I tried a couple of steps and almost pitched on my face. She took my arm. "Grab his other arm. We got to find a cop." The man was carrying a small case like musicians use for trumpets. He changed it to his other hand and felt for a dry place on my arm. Between the two of them I made the street. Ninth Avenue was still deserted. No taxis. No cops. No nothing.

"If I could just get a cab," I said.

"Fat chance this time of night in this part of town," said the man.

"There's a subway station a few blocks up," I said. "I'm sorry to bother you. I think I can make it okay now, thanks."

"We're going to find a cop," said the woman.

"Please don't bother. I'll be all right in a couple of minutes. Thanks just the same."

"Well, then, come on. You heard him," said the man. "You heard him say he's okay."

"We can't leave him like this. They may come back." I hadn't thought of that. Just then I stumbled and the man caught me from falling. He swore under his breath when he grabbed me and I couldn't blame him. I was covered with filth.

"Look, you people go on." I was starting to get all swimmy again and I didn't want to vomit in front of them. "I'll be all right. There'll be a cab along in a few minutes or a cop or something."

"Well," said the woman. "If you're sure…" Footsteps were coming around the corner. "Maybe this is a cop." But it wasn't the reassuring gleam of buttons…just another man. The woman called to him as he was walking toward us. "Say, mister. Have you seen a cop around anywhere?"

"What's the trouble?" I started to fade again. It was like the blackout in London where you couldn't see anyone's faces…just blurry shapes. We had been talking in that hushed voice you use in blackouts even though guns are slamming a few blocks over. Or maybe it was just the way I was feeling that made the voices seem hushed and far away, like a radio with a bum tube…one minute loud and the next so faint you could hardly hear anything.

"This drunk just got mugged up the street in an alley," said my savior with the trumpet case. "We was passing by and musta scared them off. You don't know where there's a hack stand around here, do you?"

"No. Can he talk?"

"I'm all right and I'm not drunk," I said. "If I could just sit down for a couple of minutes I'd be all right. There'll be a patrol car or something along in a few minutes. You go on."

"Well, you can't sit here," said the woman.

"Why don't he go to a Turkish bath?" said the last man. "Sober him up."

"Well, for Christ's sake let's get him somewhere," said the man with the horn angrily. "We can't stand around all night ya-ta-taing. Do you know where one is near here?"

"Yeah, not far. I'll take him. I'm going that way."

"Is that okay with you?" the woman asked me. Okay? It sounded like heaven. Hot water. A place to lie down. I told them so.

"Where is it?" asked the woman.

"Three up and one over."

"That's right on our way, too," she said.

"You don't have to," said the man. "I can take him okay."

"Give me your horn, Joey, and help him." And Joey did.

I don't remember much of the three up and one over except that we didn't pass a cab or patrol car or I would have done that instead. But I couldn't be sure because I was too busy concentrating on not passing out so they wouldn't have to carry me completely. As it was we had to stop every little while to give them a rest and the musician got madder and madder.

At last I could see a lighted sign up the street. Not neon. Just a bare bulb in front of a painted sign. That was Mecca. That was the Bluebird we'd been looking for. That was, when we got up to it, the *Regal Baths— Open All Night*.

"Well," said the woman. "You'll be okay now."

"I'll take him in," said the other guy. I almost started crying again when I thanked the woman and musician. I tried to pay them something but they wouldn't have it. I couldn't say any of the things I felt and of all the things I could have said, the lousy, Limey cliché "It was damn nice of you" was about the stupidest, but that's what came out.

They went on up the street melting into the darkness, and the third Samaritan helped me into the Regal Baths.

Inside the front doors, there was a counter on the left with an arched opening in the wire netting that ran from the top of the counter to the ceiling. Hanging behind it was a green-shaded drop light. The circle of light fell on stacks of wire baskets, towels and a man tilted back in a chair in the corner absorbed in, of all things, *Harper's Bazaar.* I wondered for a moment what he could find in that breathless magazine to interest him so. He didn't seem quite the type to soak his elbows in halves of lemons, not in his dirty pair of white ducks, T-shirt, grubby sneakers and no socks. But I should have guessed. Just a refined taste in pin-ups. The whole time I stood there he didn't stop staring at a particularly pneumatic underwear ad.

Everything in the place—the walls, the counter, the price list for "Baths, Massages, Sleeping Accom." wired to the fencing, even to the man with the magazine—had a film of moisture. Beads of water were forming on the low ceiling and splattering to the linoleum floor in regular pats. The air was warm and humid and was a mixture of familiar smells: sweat and soap and alcohol and liniment. I leaned against the counter watching the man staring at the magazine and wondered what to do.

There was a pay phone on the wall by the cash register, but if I called the police what could I tell them? As far as I could tell no bones had been broken and nothing stolen. I could call a cab, but by the time it came and I got back to the Casbah it would be almost five o'clock. Right now all I wanted in life was to lie down and sleep for a while and not have to make any effort or decisions. I needed a bath and my clothes cleaned but most of all I needed sleep. I pounded on the counter. The T-shirt sat up and his chair fell on its front legs. He peered at me. I hadn't seen my face but from his expression it must have been something.

"Jeez, buddy. What hit you?" He didn't get up. Just stared at me.

"I had an accident. What about a room?"

"You look bad, buddy. You ought to see the doc."

"I'm all right. Have you got a room or not?" He got up and walked over to the counter window, keeping his place in the magazine with a spongy-looking finger. He wasn't very tall. The overhead light threw shadows under his eyes and nose and emphasized his thinning hair.

"What'd you say? I'm kind of hard of hearing." I shouted my question at him twice before he got it. "Yeah. No room though. Beds. Dormitory-type, see."

"I need a shower, too, and can you do something about my clothes?"

"How long you gonna sleep?" I figured if I slept till nine I'd have time to get back to the Casbah and change before rehearsal. I told him I wanted a call at nine. "Okay. I can get 'em fixed up pretty good at the Greek's next door in the morning." I sneezed.

"Can I get a rubdown now?"

"No rubber at night. In the morning. Eight o'clock. Just leave your stuff out back. I'll pick it up." He grabbed a towel and a small cake of soap and slapped them down on the counter. He pointed to a door at the end of the hall. "Through there."

I took the soap and towel and started for the door. Then I remembered my Samaritan friend. I'd been so busy with my own problems that I'd completely forgotten about him. Fine thing. When people go to all that trouble and you just stand there with your back to them and don't even thank them.

"Did you see where my friend went?" I asked the basket man. I had to shout that a couple of times, too.

"I didn't see nobody, buddy. You come in alone."

"But he helped me in here. He was standing right there. You must have seen him."

"Hit the showers, buddy. You're getting those little men and that's bad." I suppose I should have chased my friend down the street to thank him, but I wasn't up to chasing anything. I guess some people are just nicer than other people. He didn't wait to be thanked. Now me, if I should so much as give my seat to a lady in the subway, I'd half expect to be remembered in her will, but this guy practically carries me God knows how far, gets himself all dirty from my puke and then doesn't even wait to be thanked. Yes, I guess some people are just nicer than other people.

I took my soap and towel and went through the door at the end of the hall, down another narrow hall and door and into a fair-size room. On the opposite side was a swinging half door going into a shower room. Next to it was a steam room sprouting hissing pipes. The pane of glass in the middle of the door was clouded over.

Another opening led to the room with the beds, dormitory-type, see. More green-shaded drop lights hung over a couple of rubbing tables and the worn greasy leather tops shone in the glare. An electric cabinet that had once been white was against the wall between the rubbing tables. The walls and ceiling were sheeted with elaborately embossed metal and had been painted white, but at all the corners and nail heads, rust had bled through and mottled the white with orange. A few wooden arm chairs, benches and white tables did the rest of the furnishings. On one of the long benches outside the dormitory, two naked men were putting on their shoes. I sagged into the nearest chair and sat there, too tired to begin getting undressed. Just staring at the floor.

Through the soft hissing of the pipes I heard a faint tinkle and for some reason it reminded me of the army. For a moment I half thought I was back in the army...in a hospital waiting to see the doctor...everything was going to be all right...I'd be put in a warm bed and sleep and sleep and nurses would be nice to me and no one would try to kill me anymore and I'd have a dark red bathrobe at the foot of my bed...and there was that tinkle that started all this...and it was coming from the direction of the two men. I rolled my head around and looked at them. After I got my eyes focused I could see that they were both fairly young with fish-white skins except for the faces, necks and hands, which were sun-burned, leaving a sharp dividing line at the throat and wrists. The bigger one also looked older and had a reddish appendectomy scar like a monstrous centipede crawling toward his crotch. There was also a tiny light flickering on his chest and that was what was making the familiar tinkle. He was wearing a soldier's dogtags. As he bent over to fasten his shoes, the dogtags would jingle and flash. The metal necklace shone, too. I remembered when they made us change from the cloth tape and plastic necklaces they used to issue to the metal kind. Right after the Coconut Grove fire—so you could be sure and not get the bodies mixed up. How would they have identified me if I'd been killed in the alley? That was a stupid thought…I still had my billfold. In Normandy we'd cut slices out of corrugated German gas mask tubes for binding around the edges of the dogtags so the tinkle wouldn't give you away on patrol—no need for that anymore. They had both finished putting on their shoes and were stamping about in their combat boots. Those things were so big your legs always looked puny in them.… They were both soldiers then.… Why is it that soldiers always put their shoes on first? Now they were putting on underwear—olive drab… Do they still issue olive drab?… No need for camouflage now.… Don't they know the war's over? As they lifted their pants out of the little wire baskets the one with the dogtags noticed me and called to me. It was hard to concentrate on what he was saying…the warmth…the not lying dead in an alley.

"Hey, Mac. Got the time?" I didn't have the energy to answer. He walked over to me buttoning his fly. Then he saw my face. "What hit you, Mac?" He couldn't be more than twenty.

"Accident," I mumbled.

"You can say that again, Mac. Hey, Lou, get a load of this guy." Lou came over struggling into his shirt. He whistled when he got a close-up,too. Then he laughed.

"You oughta see the other guy, huh, Mac?"

"Yeah." I tried to smile but my face was too puffed and sore.

"What time did you say it was?" I held out my wrist and they looked at my watch. "Four-fifteen. Hey, Lou, get the lead out. That bus leaves in half an hour." He clumped back to his basket. But Lou was fascinated with the condition of my face.

"How'd you do it, Mac? Fight?"

"Sort of."

"Where?" Before I could answer him a hulk of a man appeared at his side and shouldered him out of the way. I couldn't see his face, but his huge sloping shoulders seemed to be bursting out of a white underwear shirt. The light behind him through patches of fur formed an aura around his arms and shoulders that made him look even bigger. He had on soiled ducks and sneakers like the basket man. Lou glared at him, but the sheer massiveness of the guy quickly overcame any ideas Lou may have had of taking a poke at him for shouldering him out of the way. Lou went back to his dressing grumbling. The rubber picked me up like a dummy and propped me against the wall and started to take off my clothes. He was evidently used to drunks, which he must have assumed I was, because he was very efficient.

"The guy outside said he'd get these fixed up by morning," I said as he threw my clothes in a chair. He pulled off my shoes and socks as if I were a baby and then kicked a pair of wooden clogs out from under a bench and jerked his head at the showers. I slipped on the clogs, picked up the soap and towel and scuffled across the room to the showers. He followed me. His rubber soles made no noise on the linoleum.

The shower room had a row of small individual shower stalls and one gig stall for the hose. Standing under the rushing hot water felt wonderful. The rubber stood outside watching me, apparently to see that I didn't fall over. I examined as much of my body as I could see. There wasn't a mirror around. As far as I could make out, it didn't look as bad as I had expected. Bruises were starting. My face stung a little, but not too much, and there didn't seem to be any blood. I just stood under the roaring water soaking in the heat until my fingers started to shrivel. When I came out drying myself, the soldiers were still dressing. The rubber took a sheet from the cabinet and spread it on the table, then sat on a corner of it with his tree-trunk arms folded, waiting for me. The light was on his face. He'd have to have been a third-rate prizefighter for a good many years to get a face as cut up as that. One of his ears, the nearest to the light, had a cauliflower tinge. His nose was pushed in and there was a white line running from it to the top of his lips where it had once been split. It twisted his mouth like a harelip. He was, all in all, about as tough-looking a customer as I have ever seen. His puffy eyes stared at my face. I must look bad, I thought. As I came over he got up from the table and I stretched out on my stomach.

"Take it easy," I said. "I'm not feeling so good." He didn't say anything but poured some oil on my back and started rubbing. He knew his job and the long heavy strokes of those hands pushed away the soreness. I tried to think about what had happened, but the strokes began to get monotonous and I started to drift off. A slap on the buttock brought me back and indicated that I was to turn over.

I turned over and closed my eyes again. He'd finished with my chest and stomach and arms and legs and was standing at the head of the table working on my neck. That was still the sorest from the rabbit-punch. For some reason I began to think about Life Savers.... That struck me as a funny thing to be thinking about and I wondered why I should have thought of that. Then I remembered vaguely that I had wakened myself up in the alley saying it over and over again. The rubber's hands were moving slowly on the back of my neck. The fingers probing into the soreness—gently, for such an ox. My head was pressed into his stomach as he would pull my neck toward him. The oil he was using reminded me of football and basketball games when I was in school. It was cool...a nice smell, a relaxing smell...back and forth went his hands on my neck. I felt myself dozing off again...almost purring... The smell reminded me of something else, too. Something I couldn't quite remember with the smooth rhythm of his fingers on my neck. It was the smell of something like…Life Savers—and suddenly my eyes flew open. Upside down over me was the rubber's face, his puffy slits of eyes fixed on mine…watching them. I'd awoken mumbling "Life Saver" after being slammed in the face with a hand…. And the hand had smelled like…Life Savers.

The fingers on my neck were no longer soothing. I was conscious of them now as part of a hand, a hand that could be like a brick. The eyes were still staring down at me. I could see the hairs in his nose and the long, healed cuts over his eyes. I wasn't sleepy anymore. I began to get panicky. If this was the same guy—! Lying stark naked on a slab with him fingering my neck was as good a time as any to get panicky. I sat up and swung around till my feet were touching the floor. He made no effort to stop me, but he kept one huge hand on my shoulder. Maybe it was my imagination but it looked as though the packs of muscles in his shoulders were getting ready for something. He just stood there and looked at me. The cracks of his eyes glittered.

"Okay, I feel better now. That'll be all. I'll be going." I started to stand up. The hand on my shoulder didn't give and I couldn't budge.

"You got alcohol coming." Those were the first words he had spoken. It might have been the same voice that said, "Hold it. Someone's coming." I couldn't be sure. All I could be sure of was that I wanted to get the hell out of this place now. The room seemed even hotter and the glistening walls felt as though they were moving nearer. It was an effort to breathe. Sweat started running from my armpits down the side of my body.

"Never mind the alcohol," I said. "I'm going." He took a step toward me. I couldn't hear his feet on the floor. He just moved next to me. Panic started squirting up in my throat. I fought it back. I wasn't alone in an alley, this time—what was I being so chicken about? The two soldiers dressing on the other side of the room would make three against one—that was enough for even Jo-Jo, the dog-faced boy. God bless the army. Uncle Tim needs *you*.... Of course! But Jo-Jo was one thought ahead of me. My yell didn't even get a good start around the paw that was slapped over my mouth and before I knew what was happening I was flipped neatly over on my stomach and both my wrists clamped in one of his hands behind my back and being forced up toward the back of my head. I tried to bite the hand over my mouth but my teeth slipped on the grease. I tried thrashing from side to side, but he pinned me down the rest of the way with his chest. One of the soldiers must have heard part of my yell or saw me kicking my feet, the only part of me still free.

"What's eatin' ya, Mac?" he called over. The stupid son of a bitch. Why didn't he come over and find out what was eating Mac?

"Just goosey," said the rubber. His mouth was next to my ear and I knew now. It was the voice of my good Samaritan who had suggested the Turkish bath in the first place. The soldiers thought his remark was very,

very funny. Just to make sure I couldn't attract their attention again, the rubber pinched my nose together with his thumb and forefinger till I couldn't even kick anymore.

The soldiers must have finished dressing. Even through the pounding in my ears I could hear them call good-night to the rubber and me and stomp out. Only the rubber could answer. When a door slammed, he unpinched my nose and let me breathe again. In the distance I could hear the sound of a cash register and then a muffled door slam and then...quiet...except for the hissing of pipes and my struggle for breath. Still holding my arms behind my back and his hand over my mouth, the rubber straightened up. He made a noise like a chuckle.

"You need some steam," he said. "Good for you. Sober you up." He jerked me to my feet. I tried to kick him, but I slipped on the wet floor. He jolted me upright with a knee in my back. Slowly he pushed me toward the steam room. I tried hooking my leg around a table but he yanked me loose. He kicked open the door to the steam room and threw me in. I bounced on a wall and crashed on a bench. He slammed the door. I rushed at it but he had locked it and was standing with his back covering the window, I tried to grab one of the benches, but it was bolted to the floor. I hammered on the door. It was so hot when I touched it I could feel my skin burn. I tried kicking but my bare feet wouldn't budge it. I yelled and the back disappeared from the door glass. I groped around the walls frantically searching for something I could use as a weapon or to break the glass. Suddenly my hand was caught in a loop of chain which swung my arm against a scalding pipe. I tugged my arm away and the chain broke and something tinkled to the floor. The familiar tinkle of dogtags. They were at least something. Maybe I could pry the lock with them. I fumbled around on the floor for them but they had fallen into a mass of steam pipes and I only burned myself more before I had to give up trying to find them.

All at once I noticed that there was more steam and the room was getting hotter. The hissing that had been faint at first got louder and louder. I could no longer see the square light in the door. Almost-boiling water started leaking out on the floor from somewhere and I had to keep jumping from one foot to the other. I pounded on the door again and screamed, but the steam got in my lungs and I ended up in a croak. I couldn't even sit on a bench—it was red hot. I burned my hands again trying to find a cut-off switch to the steam inlet as none of the knobs I found would turn. So this was how it was going to happen to me… This was the one that had my name on it—and it wouldn't even be my name when they found me but the name on the dogtags I couldn't find in the pipes. I crouched by the door on all fours holding my head as near the floor as I could get it. The heat came lower and lower. The steam was like molten steel clogging up my nose…sliding down my throat. I crouched gasping for breath…waiting…waiting until the cloud of steam would swallow me completely.

# CHAPTER TWENTY-FOUR

SOMEONE WAS SLAPPING my face. I didn't want to open my eyes. I didn't want to face what was going to happen next.

"Hey, Mac," said a voice. "Hey, Mac, snap out of it." The slapping got harder. I opened my eyes. A soldier was slapping my face. It was the one with the dogtags. "He's coming out of it now." The face of Lou, the other soldier, bent down over me.

"You want to be careful, Mac," he said. "You could have been hurt bad."

"A damn fool thing to do," said the first soldier. "You oughtn't to fall asleep in a steam room. It ain't healthy."

"He tried to kill me," I said.

"Who tried to kill you, Mac?"

"That rubber. He locked me in that room. He tried to kill me."

"Look, Mac, you wasn't locked in no room. The door wasn't locked. Was it, Lou?"

"Hell, no. The guy's screwy." I tried to sit up and fell back down again. The two of them helped me to a sitting position. I was back on the rubbing slab. I looked at the door of the steam room. It was wide open and clouds of steam were billowing out.

"Come on, Lou," said the first soldier. "Mac's okay now. We got ten minutes to catch that bus."

"You okay, Mac?"

"For Christ's sake," I said, "I tell you he tried to kill me."

"Aw, he's still goosey," said Lou. "Come on." He started for the door.

"Wait a minute," said the first one, "this crap about someone trying to kill you, that on the level?"

"I'm trying to tell you. That rubber tried to kill me in an alley and then he locked me in the steam room."

"I told you he was screwy," said Lou. "Come on. If we miss that bus we're AWOL. You're just hungover, Mac, better go in and sleep it off."

I looked around the room. It was empty except for the three of us.

"Where's the rubber that was here?" I asked.

"How the hell should we know? Lou here forgot his dogtags. He left 'em in the steam room and we come back for 'em—and the door wasn't locked, either." He started for the door, too. "Lou's right. You better try and sleep it off...but not in a steam room. Come on, Lou."

"Wait a minute," I yelled. "Don't leave me here alone. Help me out to the street."

"Look, Mac," said the first soldier. "We got ten minutes to make the bus back to camp. We don't know nothing about you. If you say someone tried to kill you, okay, someone tried to kill you, but we're getting back to camp. So long."

"For God's sake just help me get out to the street,

won't you? That's all I want, I can get a cop there and prove it to you."

"We ain't got time to prove anything. If you want we should help you out to the street, come on. We'll hold your hand out to the street but we ain't got all day."

"Aw, leave him alone…he's nuts I tell you," said my pal Lou.

"Naw…we'll get you out to the street if that's all you want—two seconds to get into your clothes or you go out bare ass." I didn't argue. I ran across the room and got in my clothes that were still bundled on the chair. I didn't bother with socks or underwear or shirt. The soldiers watched me throwing on my clothes.

"You got it bad, Mac. You ought to give it up." Lou jammed my hat on my head and grabbed up the rest of my clothes while I was still putting on my coat, which was stiff as a board. They dragged me through the hall and as we flew past the counter the basket man yelled something after us but we didn't wait to find out what it was. The fresh air was wonderful. Lou threw my clothes at me and they both started running down the street.

"So long, Mac," Lou called back. "Be a good little boy and lay off the stuff."

"Wait a minute," I yelled after them. "I'll get a cop and prove it to you."

"Some other time, Mac." And they ran around the corner.

I tore after them for a couple of blocks but had to give it up.

I was mad. I wanted to brain the soldiers. I wanted

to brain the rubber. I wanted to hit somebody. I was the maddest I've ever been in my life. But even that wasn't mad enough to make me go back into the Regal Baths by myself. I set off to find a cop. We'd get this thing settled once and for all, I thought.

I eventually flagged a patrol car over on Eighth and told the cops my story. They did agree to come back with me, but they wouldn't let me soil the sacred precincts of their shiny patrol car, I had to hang on the outside while we drove back. We pulled up in front of the Regal Baths and one of the cops got out.

"So you think some guy tried to lock you in a steam room after he beat you up in an alley. The same guy, huh?" It was heaven just to look at that uniform...the pretty shining buttons...the beautiful badge...the city's finest... As far as I was concerned he didn't have a face— just that wonderful, wonderful, reassuring uniform.

"Yes," I said. "There were witnesses, too." He wearily pulled out a notebook.

"Okay. What are their names?" The first fine flush of reassurance began to fade. Where had I played this game before...? At the Casbah after I'd found Kendall in my room... In Lieutenant Heffran's office... Always they want names, and always I don't know them.

"I—I don't know their names."

"Oh. Well, where can we get in touch with them?" Where could we?

"I don't know that, either."

"Say, what's going on here?"

"There were two people...." I said hurriedly. "A man

and woman—he was a musician I think—and then there were two soldiers... One of them was named Lou and the other one had a big scar on his stomach...."

"That's fine. That's great." He put the book away disgustedly. "Well, come on. Let's see about the rubber guy." We entered the Regal Baths and we'd no sooner got through the doors than the basket man rushed up to us and started in.

"Where did you catch him, Officer? I was just calling the station."

"So you were just calling the station, were you?" said the cop with a suspicious look at me. "And why were you doing that?" For some reason the basket man didn't seem hard of hearing now. He answered the first time.

"This punk tried to run off without paying. He tried to run out on me."

"Oh, he did. Well, we'll get around to that later. Tell the rubber to come out here."

"What rubber?" said the basket man.

"This man says your rubber tried to cook him in the steam room."

"He's nuts. We don't have no rubber on at night. I told him that when he first come in and asked for a room. That's a buck and a half he owes me for the bed and shower."

"Come on back and I'll show you," I said to the cop. But even while we were going down the hall I knew it was no use. The room was empty. We looked in the shower stalls and the room with the beds, dormitory-type, see, even the toilets. There were a couple of padlocked clothes lockers where the basket man said the rubber that works only days kept his stuff, but there was no rubber.

"I told you he was nuts," said the basket man. "He come in drunk as a skunk and wants a bed and shower and rub. I tell him no rubber so he settled for a bed and shower and then tries to run out on me. Ask him if that ain't so. That I told him we don't have no rubber."

"Is it?" said the cop. What was the use? I said it was. "Okay, get it up. A buck and a half he says."

"So now I got to pay for almost getting killed?"

"Wise guy, eh." The cop started to look mean. "You got a fat lip, son. Maybe you'd like to go down to the station."

"Never mind. I'll pay." I handed over the money. "No charge for the steam?"

"Still punchy," said the basket man. I started to go. There wasn't much else I could do. "Wait a minute," said the basket man. "Now that you're paid up honest, I'll give you these you dropped back there."

He handed me a pair of harlequin glasses.

# CHAPTER TWENTY-FIVE

I WENT OUT INTO THE STREET still staring at the glasses the basket man had put in my hand. The cop followed me and got in the patrol car and drove off.

I got away from the Regal Baths as fast as I could— walking in the middle of the street this time.

So Bobby LeBranch had been there, too. He must have been in the alley with Jo-Jo the dog-faced boy. It had probably been Bobby's voice that had whispered, "Hold it. Someone's coming." It was all so simple now. The phone call at Peters the Dancing Boy's. "No, I tell you. You can't come up here." He probably didn't want to get nasty old blood all over his nice monk's-cloth slip-covers. The mickey in the Scotch. Jo-Jo and Bobby waiting outside Peters's since he was too finicky to let them take care of me in his apartment. Then following me till I got sick in the alley and almost finishing me then and there if it hadn't been for the musician and his girl. But Bobby was no fool. He just sent Jo-Jo around the corner after they had beat it up the alley to play Good Samaritan and be so helpful and suggest the dreamiest little Turkish bath he knew of. One the tourists hadn't discovered yet… He hadn't left the Baths at all while I was talking to the basket man…just slipped into the back and put on his working clothes. Maybe he worked there during the day, or at least had at one time. And what a really groovy way to take care of me: asleep at the switch in a steam room—who can prove anything? The motherly care with which he had washed me off first—always wash it before you cook it—it's a wonder he didn't put an apple in my mouth. And the sadistic delights of the rubdown just like the way you tickle a lobster to make him relax just before you pop him in the boiling water… And then calling in his pal Bobby through the back door to watch the final death throes through the little window. Bobby was probably shuddering with such delicious delight that he never even knew his glasses had fallen off.

What a pity the soldier forgot his dogtags—they had had to beat it out the back door before the final exquisite spasm. But it didn't matter…there was always tomorrow—or the day after—and there wasn't a goddamned thing I could do about it.

I'd been beaten up, almost roasted alive and only some blisters, bruises and scratches to show for it. Lieutenant Heffran would give me the same brush-off this time, just like this last cop. No proof… *You admit you had been drinking? How can you be sure you weren't just imagining the whole thing? Soldiers, you say? Well, who are they? What are their names? Oh, one is named Lou and the other has a scar on his belly? Well, isn't that peachy. Oh, a couple, too?…But still no names. And*

*then running out without paying your bill. Tsk, tsk, now
was that a nice thing to do. I have here a report from
Officer Pushface—good man, Officer Pushface—*here
there would be a pause for business of fingering reports.
*He says you were drunk and almost disorderly…. I'm
afraid, Mr. Briscoe, you were just imagining the whole
thing. Now why don't you go away for a nice long trip
somewhere and leave me the hell alone?*

At the moment I was so tired and frustrated and mad
that I would have been glad to believe the whole thing
was just imagination…D.T.'s…anything. But it wasn't.
I knew it wasn't.

But why? That's what I didn't get. Evidently I knew
something a lot of people didn't want me to know, or,
at least, they just thought I did. But what was I going to
do? I couldn't just say, "It's all a mistake, boys.
Honestly, fellas, I don't know a damn thing." Because
in the first place I didn't know who to say it to and you
can't go around being careful if you don't even know
who you have to be careful of. The smart thing to do
would be to get out of town before it was too late. But
I had a job—for the first time in months—and I was
damned if I was going to run from something now. Particularly when I didn't even know what it was.

I took a cab to the Casbah, showered and shaved as
well as I could around the scratches. I put Mercurochrome on the cuts and Band-Aids on top of that and
my face looked like a camouflage net for snowy terrain.
I knew how to treat the blisters on my hands and feet,
so I wasn't worried about them, but what the hell was

Frobisher going to say when he got a load of my patch-work puss, particularly since he'd come right out and told us that the only reason Maggie and I were in the show was to look pretty, and scabs and Band-Aids don't do anything for you.

I wondered for a moment if he could fire me. This was no act of God…this was an act of that bastard Bobby. And to get fired on top of everything that had happened to me last night would be the last straw.

But what happened to me last night wasn't going to happen to me again, not if I could help it. I hadn't done so well with my bare hands, so from here on in I was going to have a gun, gun-control laws notwithstanding. The law had been conspicuously absent last night when I could have used it, so the law could just shove it.

My German pistol, which was almost standard equip-ment for every G I veteran of the war, was still in a shoe at the bottom of my closet. Bobby must have found the Youth and Beauty Book that time before he got as far as looking in my shoes. There was still too much oil in the barrel and it would never have passed an inspection, but there wasn't time to do anything about that now. It would shoot. The clip was still loaded and the click as I shoved it into place was mighty comforting. I always figured I'd hock it when I got completely broke, but never quite did. The S.S. Major who owned it originally and I had played a very interesting scene in which the pistol was an important prop, and I was kind of proud of my performance.

I got dressed and wrapped the pistol in a handkerchief and put it in my breast pocket. It pulled my coat down on the right side, though by experimenting in the mirror I found that if I kept my hand in the right pants' pocket, it wasn't so noticeable.

Well, that seemed to be all. As I closed and locked my door I thought to myself how nice it was there was nobody around to say, "This is it!", an expression that always made me want to retch.

But I must admit that as I went down the steps and out into the street it was what I was thinking.

I didn't even stop for breakfast at Riker's. I was taking no chances today. The last time I had had coffee and eggs some very unpleasant things happened soon after. Let's face it—I was scared. Every man on the street was a potential Bobby and he wouldn't even be wearing his fancy glasses now to help identify him. I had them hidden behind the baseboard at the Casbah. While I waited for the subway I hugged the walls of the station. I stayed on the local. It was too easy to get pushed accidentally on purpose in front of a subway train. You think about those things after someone you don't know deliberately tries to kill you.

I'm so conditioned by the movies that I half expected during the walk up from Times Square to be shouldered into a waiting black sedan and whisked away for the final chase, and I sighed with relief when the Lyceum stage door came into view.

Almost the entire company was standing around on the sidewalk getting a few final gulps of fresh air before rehearsal on the dusty stage. I pulled my hat down farther over my face and tried to make the stage door before anyone noticed me, but it didn't work. Showers grabbed my arm and pulled me back on the sidewalk.

"Can such things be?" he declaimed, hamming it up with gestures. "And overcome us like a summer's cloud without our special wonder." I tried to shake him off, but then Miss Randall joined in.

"I pray you speak not. He grows worse and worse." Which was no lie. I was getting mad. "Question enrages him. At once good night. Stand not upon the order of your going, but go at once…" With all that, even I could recognize the quotation now. Banquo's ghost scene from Macbeth. It had been in Kendall's unfinished letter to Bobby, but I didn't have time to think about it now, I was too busy trying to dream up a plausible story. I couldn't tell them the truth…. Why should they believe me any more than the cops? And even if they did, I'd probably get fired. Mr. Frobisher certainly wouldn't want valuable rehearsals interrupted with someone trying to kill one of his bit players all the time. The show must go on! As it was, Mr. Frobisher was about as frantic as he could get with the story I did whip up. Lord knows what he would have done with the truth, probably busted a gut.

I made up a story about stumbling down some stairs and scratching myself on a plaster wall and a few doors that happened to be around. The whoops of laughter this brought from the rest of the cast didn't make me feel any better, either. I was glad that Maggie wasn't there yet because she would undoubtedly shut them up by telling them the whole thing, or as much as she knew and I didn't want that...not yet.

Mr. Frobisher kept cross-examining me. Wanted to know where the stairs were, exactly how it had happened—had I seen a doctor? I must be careful the cuts didn't get infected. Those things can be dangerous. He was telling me! I told him I had put the stuff on myself but he would have none of it.

"You go see my doctor now." He wasn't asking—he was telling. "We're starting with the first act so you'll have time. I don't want you to take a chance, Tim...I know what can happen." He got an odd look in his eye and I knew what he was remembering so I asked him for the address and started to go.

Just then two cabs pulled up and getting out of the first one was old Square-Mouth, Margo. She had certainly taken me at my word. Libby had made me promise to introduce Margo to Mr. Frobisher when I was definitely set and Margo was holding me to it. All that business about her wanting to act being Libby's idea was a lot of whoop-de-doo. Even though judging by Frobisher's fatherly interest in my scratches I was in pretty solid, I still didn't want to annoy him with women getting over divorces by going into the theater. But there didn't seem to be any way out of it. I had promised.

"Mr. Frobisher," I said. "I'm terribly sorry to bother you, but a friend of mine would like to see you about an understudy job." And before he had a chance to refuse I called Margo over. She was just finished paying off the cab and at least had the good grace to pretend she was surprised to see me there. She came over very reluctantly but she didn't need to overdo it. A dark fur coat softened that Bennington look today and as far as type went she wasn't too much of an impossibility to understudy Miss Randall after all. But Mr. Frobisher wasn't buying any.

"I'm sorry, Mr. Briscoe, but I don't make it a practice to interview people on street corners." He turned on his heel and stalked through the stage door. Two minutes ago I was *Tim* and mustn't take a chance getting my little cut infected and now I was *Mr. Briscoe* and I could drop dead. That's what happens when you try to help someone.

"Whew," I whistled after he'd gone. "I'm sorry, Margo, but I tried."

"It doesn't matter." But I could tell that it did. No woman likes to be cut dead on the street. "I had no business imposing on you this way. It was all Libby's idea really. Thanks for trying, anyway. But what happened to you? Were you in an accident?"

"Yeah, I'll tell you all about it sometime, but I've got an appointment right now. So long."

"Perhaps I can drop you off."

"No thanks, Margo, I'd rather walk."

"Okay, well thanks again." She started for the cab still standing at the curb. I remembered something I had meant to do.

"Just a minute, Margo." I reached into my pocket and pulled out a five-dollar bill and walked over and put it in her hand. She looked down at it in surprise.

"What's this for?"

"The theater tickets the other night."

"Oh...but..."

"Now don't argue."

"But I don't understand what this is all about."

"I'm not sure I do myself." Greg Moulton, the stage manager, had just come out the stage door to herd the rest of the cast in. Well, since I'd started being the little Boy Scout, I might as well finish the job. Besides, who was Frobisher to get so high and mighty? He'd been nothing but a stage manager himself not so many years ago.

"Greg, would you mind coming here a minute?" He came over. "I'd like you to meet Margo Shaw. I think she might be a good bet for understudy. I wish you'd introduce her to Frobisher." Greg looked her over.

"Well, you might fit the clothes, at that, Miss Shaw, but you understand with a star like Miss Randall there's not much chance of your going on even if she does get sick."

"She understands all that, but you know Frobisher always has understudies, star or no star. The least you can do is let him decide."

"Well, why don't you come back in about an hour, Miss Shaw, and I'll introduce you to him during one of the breaks. Okay?"

"That's terribly nice of you," said Margo. She seemed a little amused. I guess she could afford to be a little amused about getting a seventy-five-buck-a-week job— if she could wear a coat like that one. "But I don't think..."

"Nuts," I said. "What can you lose? Go have lunch and be back at two. It's all set." I opened the door to the cab and there was Maggie sitting in the back. She'd evidently been there the whole time watching me be noble. She got out and Margo got in and drove off.

"What's the idea of sitting in that cab all this time spying on me?"

"Oh, Timmy, I wasn't spying on you. I was waiting for all those people to go away so you could tell me what happened. Darling, who hurt you…was it Bobby—did he try to kill you? Oh, Timmy, we're not going to wait another minute. Come on—we'll go to the police.…"

"Now calm down, Maggie. It was just an accident. I'm perfectly all right. Just a few scratches…"

"But how did it happen? You're lying to me. They tried to kill you."

"I'm not lying and nobody tried to kill me. Stop being so hysterical." What was the use of upsetting her? It wouldn't do any good. There wasn't anything she could do about it now. So I told her approximately the same story I told the rest of the cast. She, at least, didn't laugh. But I'm not sure she believed me, although she pretended to.

"Then you're really all right?" I assured her I was. "Well, that's good, but don't ever scare me again like that. Oh, Timmy…wait till you see my dress. It is absolutely out of this world. Ernie and Jenny did themselves proud. I only hope it isn't too good or Miss Randall will never let me wear it. And Ernie made the most marvelous little hat to match—"

"Never mind about your dress, did you go to Chorus Equity?"

"I'm sorry, Timmy, but I'm afraid I overslept."

"Then you didn't go?"

"In a word, no."

"Then you've got time to do it now."

"But what about rehearsal? We're late already."

"Frobisher sent me to the doctor's and they are starting with the first act so it will be at least an hour, and don't forget I offered you a drink out of the office bottle when you did it."

"Okay, chief, but you're a hard man. Maybe I'll try and get a job at Chorus Equity. You'll be sorry when I'm dancing in a *louche* dive in South America."

"See if you can get one for me, too. I'll probably need it after today."

Frobisher's doctor had his office in Radio City and Frobisher's name got me right in without an appointment. While the doc was cleaning out my scratches Frobisher even called up to check on my condition. With at least a hundred thousand dollars already invested in the play I could understand why he would want to make sure that my part as a walking cocktail shaker wasn't going to look like a class in first aid. The doc reassured him that I would look reasonably human in a couple of days but I didn't feel that his final tape job was much of an improvement over mine.

I was about a hundred yards from the Lyceum when I saw him. Just seeing my dog-faced pal, Jo-Jo, again was like a kick in the stomach. I ducked into the doorway of a Mexican restaurant and watched him through the angle of the window glass. He stood for a moment looking up and down the street. Even at that distance he looked big. Big and ugly. My throat was dry and I was scared. Even with a gun I was scared. Jo-Jo slowly lit a cigarette, then packed those huge hands in his pockets and shuffled off toward Broadway. I transferred the pistol to my coat pocket and started to follow him. I didn't know what I was going to do if I did catch up to him, and when I got to Broadway I was almost relieved that I lost him in the crowd. What was he doing in the Lyceum? Had he come back to finish the job he'd started on me last night? God, if he was being that open about it… If he was that set on killing me…he'd be back in a little while to try again, and maybe better luck next time—and I knew there would be a next time and a next time after that until he did it. Or I did it. Bobby was playing for keeps. No picking up your marbles and going home when you got bored with this game. I was sick at myself for being glad that Jo-Jo had disappeared in the crowd. I'd had my chance…even a gun. I could have forced him to go with me to Lieutenant Heffran…or I could have even shot him in the back. This was no time to be concerned about ethics. But now I'd have to wait until he came at me again. At his convenience…and he would choose the place—and there are an awful lot of choice places in New York. Alleys, subways, rooming houses, Turkish baths…even backstage in theaters… All my life I've been avoiding them, but now it looked as though Mr. Milquetoast was going to have to make a choice—either just wait for it to happen where or when Bobby wanted, or go out and look for it and make it happen. And when I thought this over on the way back to the theater I realized that I hadn't much of a choice after all. The decision was just about made for me.

Maggie was waiting in the hall.

"What did the doctor say, Tim? Are you going to live?"

"At least the scratches won't kill me, if that's what you mean."

"Of course that's what I mean. What did you think I meant?"

"It doesn't matter, Maggie. I was just trying to be funny."

"Well, I don't like you being funny like that." She looked my face over very carefully. "Are you sure you're all right? You look sort of odd."

"I'm okay. Maggie, how long have you been standing here in the hall?"

"About ten minutes. Why?"

"Did you see someone go out just now? A big guy?"

"Looked like an ape?"

"That's the one."

"Yes. Friend of yours?"

"Did he ask for me?"

"No. He just left. Maybe you can still catch him."

"Thank you, no."

"Well, he'll probably come back," said Maggie.

"Yes," I said, "he probably will. What did you find out at Chorus Equity?"

"Oh, Timmy. What a place. It reminded me of Polly Adler's in all its glory."

"How do you know what Polly Adler's looks like?"

"Don't be so literal. Besides, I have gentlemen friends. Anyway, they wouldn't tell me if they had a Bobby LeBranch in their files because I didn't have sense enough to tell them I was doing bumps in some musical, so I got one of the cuties out in the hall by the elevator to go in. It really is the most amazing place. You've never seen such people. Imagine having the energy to paste on false eyelashes at this hour in the morning. Does pink hair send you?"

"Never mind about the hair. What did you find out about Bobby?"

"I'm coming to that, but most of them had pink hair, a very peculiar shade. Maybe I should try it. My little pal told me she did it herself. I wonder if I could? Or maybe you could help me with the back bits. It would probably make all the difference in my life."

"Maggie, for God's sake…"

"Don't get so excited or you'll blow a bandage. I've got it right here, Bobby's forwarding address." She fished around in her handbag. "Though I don't think it's going to do us any good because in a way we knew it all the time and Choo-Choo or Chug-Chug or whatever her name is thinks I'd do well as a showgirl and I wouldn't even have to dance…just walk around. She even offered to introduce me to Billy Rose. She's been a chorus girl for five years and knows all about it. She said I'd love it. Do you suppose I would?" She finally pulled a piece of paper out of her bag, "Here it is."

I grabbed it, straightened it out and read Choo-Choo

or Chug-Chug's florid backhand. Bobby LeBranch c/o Nellie Brant, Shubert Bldg., West 44th Street, New York City, New York.

Round and round it goes, where it stops nobody knows. We were right back where we started. I sagged down on the dressing room steps and sat staring at the crumpled bit of paper. What was the use.

Maggie sat down beside me and put her arm around me.

"You know what you ought to do, Timmy."

"Yeah, shoot myself and get it over with."

"You see. That's what I mean. What you need is to relax. You ought to get a massage or a rubdown or something." That jerked me to my feet.

"What do you mean I ought to get a massage? Why did you say that?"

"There, you see. You're so jumpy. It would do you good."

"Why do you say that?"

"Lots of actors do. It's the most soothing thing in the world."

"Maggie, what made you think of that? It's important. What made you think of a massage just now?"

"Well, look at the way you're acting. You're all tied up in knots."

"No, no. Now think, Maggie. Why did you say that just now? Please, Maggie, think back."

"I don't know.... Please, Timmy, you're hurting me." I hadn't realized that I was gripping her shoulders as hard as I could. Almost trying to shake it out of her. I let go. "Did it have anything to do with that big ape that was here a few minutes ago? The one I asked you about?"

"Why yes, Timmy. That was it. How did you know? Though I do think you could find a little nicer-looking one…he was a trifle too Neanderthal for my tastes."

"But how did you know he was a rubber—did you talk to him?"

"No, it was because they wouldn't pay their bill…."

"Because who wouldn't pay whose bill? Maggie, for God's sake tell me."

"I can't see what you're getting in such a sweat about, it wasn't your bill…I just happened to hear him trying to collect for a massage he had given last night and somebody wouldn't pay."

"Who wouldn't pay?"

"Darling, how should I know? I was just waiting out here for you to get back from the doctor's and I overheard Sweetie-pie demanding his money."

"Who was he talking to?" It had to be Bobby or at least a friend of Bobby's and he was in the theater ten minutes ago…. Maybe he was still here. "Who, Maggie? Who?"

"Oh, darling, I'm afraid I didn't see him. You see I was standing over there by the door that goes onstage and I just overheard them. It isn't nice to eavesdrop I know, but I just happened to be standing there…I didn't mean to listen, really. If I'd known it was so important I could have looked in, but how was I to know?"

"But what did the person he was talking to sound like…could you recognize his voice? Think back."

"No, I'm sorry. You know how it is…all sort of muffled, and actually I could only hear Sweetie-pie clearly and I'm afraid I wasn't paying much attention. Did it have something to do with you-know-who?"

"'Sweetie-pie,' as you call him, was probably talking to Bobby when you heard him. That's all."

"Oh, Timmy, no. But why didn't you tell me? You mean he's here in the theater?"

"It's either Bobby or one of his buddies. Did anyone leave after Sweetie-pie?"

"No, I'm sure of that, though you can get out through the front of the house if you want to. Oh, Timmy, I'm sorry if I messed it up, but you don't tell me everything and how was I to know?"

"It isn't your fault…I never dreamed he'd come here. Come on, let's go in and try and see if you can spot the voice you heard—you follow me around and give me a nudge at the slightest suggestion of the same voice."

"I'll try, but I'm afraid it's not much use. Sweetie-pie did all the talking, but let's go. Only do be careful. Things are forever happening to people backstage."

"Just what do you mean by that?"

"Well, you know…in the movies…things falling out of the flies on top of people…the Phantom of the Opera…you know."

She would have to bring that up at a time like this.

# CHAPTER TWENTY-SIX

WHEN WE GOT ON THE STAGE it looked like old home
week. I didn't even know where to begin. Ernie had
brought over a hat for Miss Randall to try on. Jenny had
some swatches for curtain material for the third act she
wanted Mr. Frobisher to okay so they were having a
break. Margo was sitting in a corner by the switchboard
waiting for Mr. Frobisher to get through with Jenny so
Greg could introduce her to him properly through
channels. And Greg was talking to none other than my
old nemesis, Ted Kent. Word must have gotten around
about my accident and the old ghoul was there trying
to get my part. Yes, Libby was there, too, standing
behind him. The old double play: Margo to Libby, Libby
to Ted. Don't write or telegraph, just tell an actor. The
news will get there twice as fast. Although I had more
important things to do, I couldn't resist the opportunity.
I sauntered over to Ted, followed by Maggie, who had
somewhat the air of a birddog poising to point.

"Hello, Ted, how good of you to come," I said as
archly as I could which considering the bandage handi-
cap was pretty arch indeed. "I hate to be the one to tell

you your trip was for naught, but my physician assures me I shall be able to open with the show." I glanced at Libby. "Contrary to what you may have been told." Libby at least had the decency to blush and splutter a bit.

"Don't be ridiculous, old man," said Ted. "Libby and I just happened to be having lunch with Jenny, and she insisted we stop by here just a minute with her. I haven't quite descended to walk-ons yet. As a matter of fact…"

"Oh, Tim…" Libby fancied herself oil on troubled waters. "I think it was grand of you to arrange for Greg to introduce Margo to Frobisher."

"But, Libby," said Margo, "I still don't think I've had enough experience."

"Don't be silly, dear. You don't have to have any experience to be an understudy for a star. You never get to play it anyhow." Libby turned to me. "By the way, Tim, what did happen to you? Your face, I mean?"

"I'll tell you all about it one day." I didn't feel up to repeating my pat little story again. "Greg, how long do you think it will be before we get to the third act?"

"'Bout an hour, I should think."

Well, all four of them had said something and no nudge from Maggie. With Maggie still pattering after me I did the rounds and made an excuse to talk to everyone else on the stage. Showers still thought my accident was hilarious but didn't rate a nudge. Frobisher said he was glad I was going to be able to open. No nudge. Jenny shrieked with laughter and said my face gave her an inspiration for a new plaid, but no nudge from Maggie and I had to restrain myself from doing more than nudging Jenny and her crummy jokes.

I borrowed a cigarette from Maggie and while I was lighting it I whispered to her to meet me in the ladies' room at the front of the house right away and I wandered to the other side of the stage hoping I didn't look as keyed up as I felt. I watched Maggie go through the pass door and up the aisle to the front of the house and I gave her a couple of minutes' start, then followed her up the opposite aisle. She was waiting for me in the ladies' room when I got there.

"Well this is certainly a novel place for a rendez-vous," she said. I carefully looked in all the toilet stalls before I answered her. They were empty.

"I thought it would be the safest place. Everyone else uses the johns backstage. Well, I take it you didn't recognize any of the voices."

"But I told you I didn't hear whoever Sweetie-pie was talking to…just a mumble. I didn't think it would do any good. And those silly questions you asked. They'll think you're mad as a hatter. 'Do you think it's going to rain, Miss Randall?' and 'Do you like baseball, Mr. Showers?' *Really!*"

"Well, I had to get them to talk somehow."

"Okay. Now what do we do?"

"I've got to think."

"Is this where you come when you want to think?"

"Maggie, what do we know that Bobby doesn't want us to?"

"Not much. It's what we *don't* know that would fill a book…and I don't mean Youth and Beauty."

"Yeah, but it couldn't be the Youth and Beauty Book. He's got that back."

"All but that one page, of course."

"What do you mean, all but one page?"

"That page with our names on it. It seemed silly leaving it in that day when we were going to pitch it back in Nellie's office."

"And you tore it out?" I should have known. Maggie and her habit of tearing out pages. She nodded, very pleased with herself. "But where is it now?"

"Up in my apartment. I can get it for you if it's as important as all that. After all it didn't have anything on it but the names, did it?"

"But that must be it. That's what he's still after. Maggie, why didn't you tell me?"

"But I thought you knew. You were right there when I did it. Or weren't you? Anyway, I'm sure I've still got it."

That was it. The missing page was the missing link. That was why Bobby and Jo-Jo tried to stew me in my own juice. That was why a tombstone in New Jersey read Amos Slattery. And if I could only work it right, that would be why another tombstone would read Bobby LeBranch. That page could set up Bobby for me on my own terms. I started getting all hopped up inside. No more hugging walls in subway stations afraid I'll be pushed in front of a train. No more chairs under my doorknob. We'd get it settled once and for all. By now I could practically hear background music of the

William Tell Overture. I was Popeye after a dose of spinach. I was Dick Tracy in spades. As a matter of fact I was a damn fool, but you don't always know those things at the time.

"Maggie. How are you feeling?"

"I like that. How are *you* feeling?"

"Remember a couple of days ago you said that if I ever got anything definite about this murder business, you thought it would be sheer heaven to play cops and robbers?"

"But, angel, what bliss. Am I to be the bait for your trap?" That jolted me.

"What trap?"

"Darling, don't tell me you haven't got a trap. That's ridiculous, you must have a trap. How else can I be the bait? Could you give me time to get my hair pink? Chug-Chug says…"

"Never mind about Chug-Chug. How are you on ad-libbing? Do you have to have your lines written out for you or can you make them up as you go along?"

"I don't know. Whatever for?"

"Because in a few minutes you and I are going to play a scene in front of the whole company."

"Wonderful. Are there cocktails in it or do I really get a chance to act?"

"You get a chance to act. The idea is to bring Bobby over to your house to play by letting him know that you have the missing page to the Youth and Beauty Book."

"But what's the idea? Then Bobby *is* one of the

company? I knew it. Which one? Frobisher, Greg, Showers…? Oh, tell me."

"I'm not sure myself yet, but the less you know the safer you'll be, but I do know that if he isn't—someone in the company does know him and will pass the word along. I'm going to drop this page from the Burns Mantle *Best Plays* that you tore out at the library and then you can pick it up and sort of read through the cast aloud…. You know actors always love to talk about old plays, and then when you come to Bobby's name you can bring it in that you have seen that name before in an engagement book and you just happen to have that page at home, and what a coincidence. You don't need to mention the Youth and Beauty Book by name. Our pal will know. Then I'll take it from there. It won't make much sense to the rest of the people, but we're only playing to one person—think you can do it?"

"My God, I certainly have all the exposition in this lousy play. Why don't I just have a feather duster and say to the butler, 'I sye, 'ow careless of young Mawster Bobby to leave a page of the Youth and Beauty Book lyin' around careless like with Poor Miss Nellie not cold in her gryve!' I hope you're not planning to put money in this turkey. It doesn't look to me like it's got a prayer."

But it had to have a prayer. Now or never. Last night proved that. If I didn't get him—he'd get me. Simple as that.

"But they were wrong about *Tobacco Road.*" She sighed. "Okay, what else do I do?"

"Then you simply go home and lock your door and wait."

"Where will you be?"

"Bobby will think I am at the tailor's, I hope."

"And will you be?"

"No."

"Oh." She thought this over for a minute. "And will dreamy Bobby show up?"

"No."

"Well, it sounds like a lively afternoon for me I must say."

"Someone may phone you, though. He'll probably say it's the wrong number or something, just to see if you're home. That's the only reason I've got to have you in on this. But don't worry, he'll never get as far as your apartment."

"Is there going to be a lot of shooting? I should hate that."

"Why did you say that?"

"Well, you're sagging like an old woman on your right chest and I've certainly seen enough movies to know what that means." I must have taken my hands out of my pocket without thinking.

"Do you think any of the rest noticed it?"

"They'd be pretty damn stupid if they didn't." That set me back a bit.

"Well, it's too late now. We'll just have to take a chance. Good luck."

"'Hear it not, Duncan, for it is a knell,'" she quoted, "'that summons thee to heaven or to hell.'"

"Don't you know better than to do that?" I said angrily.

"What?"

"Quoting Macbeth...it's bad luck."

"Oh, nonsense. What a silly lot you actors are. Come on, let's get started. I can't wait." She started back up the stairs. All at once I knew it was no good.

"Wait a minute, Maggie."

She stopped and turned around. "Now what?"

"The whole thing's off. It's folded...closed out of town."

"What do you mean?"

"I'm a damn fool to even think of trying to pull a stunt like this. Just forget the whole thing."

"But you can't back out now. I don't know what it is really, but whatever it is you can't get me all excited like this and then stop."

"Not only can, but have," I said. "Let's go back." I started up the stairs.

"Now hold on a minute. What's happened? You were so excited about it a minute ago. What's changed?"

"It's too dangerous, that's all. I don't understand enough about these things to take the chance."

"Do you know enough to go to Lieutenant Heffran yet?"

"No."

"Are you just going to keep on being beaten up until they finish the job on you?"

"How did you know I was beaten up? Who told you?"

"Nobody had to tell me. But you don't think for a minute I believed that story about you falling down stairs, do you? And you've been jittery all day. Don't forget, Pistol Packin' Papa, I've known you a long time.

I've been waiting for you to tell me the truth, but when you didn't I gathered it was because you wanted to spare me the gory details. You weren't home all last night—I called you a dozen times—and then you turn up this morning looking like Hamburger Heaven... What else could I think? Now if it's yourself you're worrying about—okay. Just say so and it's all off, but if you're suddenly getting all Galahad and worrying about me—why, forget it. I don't know anything anybody could get too unhappy about—you've seen to that, dammit—so I can't imagine what could happen to me. If you want me to wait at home for a phone call and that will help any, what are we waiting for? So something should happen... What the hell, I've seen everything." She reached up and touched the bandages on my forehead lightly. "But I'm not going to have people doing things like that to you. I like you the way you are. I didn't sweat out four years of war waiting for you to come back all in one piece to let anybody try to change you all over to suit them now." I put my arms around her and kissed her. I could feel her body shiver. She pushed me away, turning her head so I couldn't see her face and ran up the stairs. But I knew she was crying.

I waited a minute then slowly followed her. Just as I came out of the ladies' room, Ted Kent came out of the men's room. He stared at me.

"Well, what do you know." He smiled and shook his head. I didn't say anything, but walked on up the stairs. He followed me, laughing to himself.

# CHAPTER TWENTY-SEVEN

AT A QUARTER TO FOUR Maggie was in her apartment and I was downstairs in the hallway inside her front door. Through the glass I could see the line of mailboxes with the buzzers you press and then wait for the tenant to push the clicker in his apartment to release the front door. I got set beside the stairway by the basement where it was darkest. There were no lights in the hall and what light there was came from Fifth Avenue through the glass in the door. I tested it first from the front. You couldn't see much in the back if you were out by the buzzers and mailboxes.

Oh, yes, it had all worked out very cleverly. Our little scene in front of the company went off without a hitch except for the fact that when I started to play drop the handkerchief with the page from Burns Mantle's *Best Plays,* ever helpful Ted Kent picked it up before Maggie could get to it, but she snatched it away from him and got on with the plot. I made it quite clear to everyone that I had to go immediately after rehearsal to a fitting at the tailor's for my new dinner jacket. Of course, if anyone had thought real hard, he would have realized

that my chances of getting a dinner jacket built in only
a few days were less than negligible, but I had to take a
chance on that. Maggie came through with flying colors
and everyone else picked up all the cues I had hoped
they would. It ended up with Maggie promising to go
home and get the page from the engagement book for
me and bring it to the rehearsal at Frobisher's apartment
that evening.

The minute the rehearsal was over I beat it out the
door, leaving Maggie and Ted and Margo and Jenny and
Libby and the rest of the cast still on the stage. I took
up my post in Maggie's hall and Maggie didn't even see
me when she came in and took the elevator up to her
apartment about twenty minutes later.

The one thing that worried me was that Maggie
would be all alone. However, I was determined Bobby
wouldn't get past the front hall. I had a pretty good idea
of what he must look like and there wouldn't be many
people coming in this time of day who didn't live in the
apartment house. He certainly wouldn't have a key. If I
had guessed right he wouldn't know that Maggie had
anything to do with my chase until this afternoon. So he
would have to push the buzzer. No little Jan lived here.

He might do the old trick of pushing someone else's
buzzer to get the door open, but I figured that any guy
that pushed would be a likely candidate and I'd have a
little talk with each one before he got in the elevator or
set foot on the stairs under which I was hidden. When
I spotted him for sure, it was just a question of sticking
my gun in his ribs and leading him to the nearest cop

and then on to smarty-pants Heffran. If he wanted to get tough, the customary thing is, I believe, a slap across the chops with the pistol. If he brought any of his playmates with him—old Jo-Jo the rubber, or Peters, the dancing boy—so much the better. I'd shoot them if I had to and explain it later. Humphrey Bogart was a sissy compared to me. I was taking no chances this time.

I stood there and smoked like a chimney trying to keep calm. Each time I lit a cigarette I ducked my head behind the stairs so the flare of the lighter wouldn't be seen from the door. After fifteen of the longest minutes on record, the mailman came and unlocked all the little boxes and put some letters in them and locked them up again and left. I waited some more.

After another couple of years, a dumpy middle-aged woman in a squashed brown hat and a squashed brown coat appeared on the other side of the glass and pushed a buzzer. Almost immediately the clicker clicked. She opened the door and instead of taking the elevator walked up the stairs. When she reached the second floor I could hear her being greeted and a door slam. In a few minutes another woman, dressed for the street, walked down the stairs, opened the door, unlocked the mailbox, took out a letter, locked the box again and walked off. There didn't seem to be much doubt that she had been relieved by the babysitter and was off to wherever it is that women go at four o'clock in the afternoon.

There was another lull during which I looked at my watch every second on the second. My palms kept dripping and I kept wiping them off on my trousers. Another woman appeared on the other side of the door and pushed a button. Presently the clicker clicked and she came in and started walking up the stairs, too. I should look into this babysitting racket…maybe I'd been wasting my time in the theater.

Suddenly the door behind me opened and a man came out of the basement. He was silhouetted against the light and I couldn't see his face. I jumped back and grabbed on to the gun in my pocket. He stood facing me. Very carefully he reached inside the door he had just come out of and switched off the basement light. I could see his face better. He wore a hat and coat. He closed the door behind him. And then I recognized him. It was the building superintendent. He knew who I was, too, and smiled.

"How you been?" he said.

"Oh, fine, fine," I replied. I certainly didn't want to get into a great conversation with him at this point. "I'm waiting for Mrs. Lanson."

"She gotten locked in any more bathrooms?" He gave me an enormous wink.

"Not that I know of." I tried to keep one eye on the front door.

"Well, take care of yourself," he said and went on upstairs.

I mopped my hands and forehead.

Then I had an idea. What if Mr. LeB. was waiting outside to see who came in. Maybe he'd seen me, but I didn't think my timing could be that far off. I was the first one to leave the Lyceum. Anyway, I might as well have a look around.

I started toward the door, but before my hand touched the doorknob, the clicker started clicking. It startled me like an electric shock. I sprang back and almost yelled. It clicked again. There was no one by the buzzers and I hadn't taken my eyes from them even while I was talking to the superintendent.

I heard a door open upstairs and someone call down. "Who is it?" I didn't say anything. The voice called again. "Is that you, Madge?" It was a woman's voice. She started walking down the stairs still calling "What do you want?" getting more and more peevish as she got near the bottom. She came all the way down and looked out through the door then turned around and saw me standing there looking as foolish as I felt. "Did you ring my buzzer just now, 3-D?" she demanded. I said I hadn't. "Well, how long have you been here?" I told her a few minutes. "Then did you see anyone ring my buzzer?"

"There was a woman who did ring for someone about a minute ago, but she went upstairs."

"Did she have white hair with a green dress?"

"I didn't notice her face."

"Well, you can remember if she had on a green dress and coat, can't you?"

"No, I think she had on a fur coat and her dress was a sort of red." I couldn't remember it clearly. The light was behind people coming in the door.

"You're sure it wasn't a green dress? Madge might have worn her fur coat but she told me definitely she would wear her green. You're sure?" I tried to remember exactly. Yes, I was sure.

"I'm sure it was a red dress. I noticed it when she started up the stairs. Sort of a funny color red."

"Oh bother," said the woman. "I'm going to speak to the superintendent. You never can tell who's running around this place. I never did approve of those buzzers anyway. They ought to have a doorman…the rent they charge." She grumbled to herself all the way back to the elevator and up and out of sight. I went back to my post and lit another cigarette. I was getting disgusted with myself. I thought I'd been so smart—that it couldn't fail, but it looked like it had.

And then, of course, it hit me. The original slow-take kid, that's me. I was the smart one…old J. Edgar Briscoe. I didn't even have sense enough to realize what had happened. It was like the Life Saver business at the bath. The funny-color red dress and the clicking buzzer—but for the wrong apartment. I finally caught on and dashed upstairs. What a fool I'd been. By God if something had happened to Maggie…

I was completely bushed when I made the fifth floor and pounded on Maggie's door. There was no answer. I pounded again and again no answer. I still had a key so I unlocked the door and kicked it open. All the blinds were down and I couldn't see anything. I called out for Maggie but nothing happened. She couldn't have left. I had the pistol in my hand and very carefully entered the foyer. I kept calling…still no answer.

He must have been hiding in the coat closet in the

foyer. He simply waited for me to walk past, then sneaked up behind me and with an umbrella from the closet neatly sliced me across the wrist of the hand holding the pistol. While I was doubled up in pain, he picked up the gun.

In the dimness, I first saw the gleam of the muzzle. No matter how dark it is you can always see a gun that's pointed at you. Through the red mist of pain from my wrist, I gradually made out what was behind the gun. A mink coat open at the front now showing a dirty magenta dress—unmistakably Ernie's creation. A thin white face with a red square mouth. Black eyes shining in the faint reflected light. A mink hat with black hair showing underneath. One gloved hand still holding the umbrella—the other the gun. It was Libby's stage-struck friend, square-mouth Margo—the gal I'd just given five dollars to a few hours earlier. It was also, I realized now, too late, the guy I'd been looking high and low for—Mr. Bobby LeBranch.

# CHAPTER TWENTY-EIGHT

WITHOUT TAKING HIS EYES or gun from me, he reached behind him and closed the front door very softly, then nodded me toward the living room.

"Okay, Puss. In there. Get going." The pistol moved closer.

"What have you done with Maggie?" He didn't say anything. Pistol or no pistol I ran into the living room.

Maggie was lying on the couch. Her eyes were closed and she was breathing heavily. I knelt down beside her and gently felt the back of her head. She moaned softly as I touched the bump that was forming. I whirled around. He was standing in the door across the room, watching, smiling.

"By God, if you've…"

"Just what will you do, Timmy?" It gave me goose-flesh to hear him call me Timmy now. It was futile to threaten him. I was helpless. I knew it and he knew it. The whiskey decanter was on the table by the couch. I poured some into a glass and forced a few drops between Maggie's lips. She coughed and rolled her face away from me. I began to rub her wrists. I didn't know what

I was going to do, but whatever it was—and I had to do something—I didn't want Maggie unconscious when I did it. But what? Oh, I knew what you were supposed to do in these scenes. You kept the murderer talking and then somebody came in and killed him and then the curtain came down and you had your bows and then you took your makeup off and went over to Sardi's. Well, it looked like the curtain was going to come down, all right, but I was going to be in no condition to take any bows. Keep him talking. For what? Who was going to come?

There might be one chance, at least for Maggie, if I didn't louse it up like I had everything else. He hadn't killed us so far. He was waiting for something. Maybe for Maggie to come around so she would know when he killed us. It would be more fun that way—if he did wait.... Oh, Maggie darling, open your eyes. Please, dear God, make Maggie open her eyes...then maybe I could rush him so he'd get me, but maybe I could tangle him up enough so she could get away.... You can keep moving for a few seconds with slugs in you, with luck I could... Oh, Maggie, open your eyes... Maggie...Maggie...

He was still standing there, smiling.

"What are you going to do to us?" Keep him talking...say something...say anything till Maggie comes to... Maggie... Maggie... Please...

"What do you think, Timmy?"

"But Maggie doesn't know anything about this. Let her go. She doesn't understand what the whole thing is about. Anyway, it was all an accident. Nellie died accidentally. The police said so...the papers..."

"But it wasn't an accident, Timmy. I had it all planned. I meant to kill her."

"But why? What did she ever do to you?" Maggie's head was rocking back and forth. How long, oh Lord, how long?

"She wasn't a nice person, Timmy. Not at all. Much better dead. She got greedy. Oh, I didn't mind a little money now and then for buying my clothes and arranging my social engagements." There was a shorter and uglier way of saying that. "But she kept wanting more money all the time. Lots more, and when I wouldn't give her more she started threatening me. She said she could have me put in prison for draft evasion," he simpered. "That and other things. Now I couldn't have that, could I? You see my point, don't you, Timmy? As soon as someone knows something about you that you don't want other people to know and they start getting greedy, the only thing to do is get rid of them. And you know something about me now that I don't want other people, strangers that is, to know. So, you see, there's nothing else for me to do. You do understand, don't you, Timmy, dear?" He was loving this. Telling me how clever he'd been...almost squirming with delight. Maggie, for God's sake wake up. He was moving slowly toward us now. "I should have thought that after old Kendall suffered a, shall we say, unfortunate accident you would have had sense enough to stop bothering me....

"Accident...?"

"I didn't mean to kill him, really...just impair his

vision slightly.... But it was just as well, because he would probably have tried to blackmail me, too, just like Nellie, and just like you if I let you go.... I thought he was too drunk, the old sot, but he'd recognized me at the funeral when you introduced us, and he found me in your room that night I went to get Nellie's engagement book. Really, what a disgusting place you live in. Surely with your looks you could have done better than that." I felt as though I were listening to a case history in one of those medical books, the kind they have to describe in Latin.

Maggie groaned. "Ah, at last. It looks like the beautiful Maggie is joining us. I didn't mean to hit her, but she got annoying and I had to...before she'd give up that page. Most unladylike." He could even laugh at this.

Maggie opened her eyes. She gasped when she saw me bending over her.

"Oh, Timmy darling. I thought you'd never get here. It was that woman, Margo. You didn't tell me it would be a woman."

"It isn't." I indicated the dark figure standing across from us. "It's our old friend Bobby LeBranch." She stared at him.

"But...but..."

"Quite convincing, too, wasn't I, Maggie? If I do say so myself." The purring voice started to take on an edge. "Shall we go into the bedroom now, if you don't mind? So much more touching, I think, and such lovely pictures for the tabloids. Publicity is *so* important, don't you agree?" We didn't move. His voice became a rasp. "Get in there."

"Oh, Timmy," said Maggie, "what's he going to do?"

"Don't worry. It'll be all right."

"Really very simple, Maggie dear." The purr was back again. "*Crime passionel,* I believe it's called. A psychoneurotic veteran and beautiful showgirl, that's what you'll be called, you know. Both discovered locked in each other's arms like Paolo and Francesca. Even death won't part you." He moved toward us. "Now get going."

I helped Maggie to her feet. Going through the door into the bedroom I might be able to throw her to one side and make a dive for him.

"Sorry you won't be able to make the opening night of your little play, but then we can't have everything, can we? Perhaps I'll get the understudy job. Thank you so much, Tim. And now that you two will be unavailable maybe I'll get to play a part, but which shall I do, yours, Maggie, or yours, Tim? That's really quite a problem." We backed toward the bedroom door. I moved a bit so Maggie would go first, but he had anticipated that.

"No dear, let the gentleman go first. And, Timmy, be sure to stand by the bed in plain sight. I do want to make it as nearly simultaneous as possible."

"You can't get away with this, LeBranch."

"Oh, I think so. Who's to tell? Not you, nor Maggie. Certainly not Nellie or Kendall. Who, then? Libby?" He came nearer. "Ted? You didn't suspect, so why should they? Which reminds me." He reached into the pocket of his coat and pulled out a crumpled five-dollar bill and tossed it to me. I didn't try to catch it. It fell to the floor and stayed there. "I really insist on paying for my ticket after all."

"The police will be here any minute," said Maggie.

"Together with the U. S. Marines, no doubt. No, Maggie dear, I'm sure we won't be disturbed."

Maggie and I had backed up until we were stopped by the bed. He reached over and snapped on the bedside radio. He had planned this scene very thoroughly. We waited forever until the radio warmed up and music blared out. He raised his voice.

"So helpful, don't you think, for covering the sound of shots." He was panting with excitement. "Really, radio is a wonderful invention. What a shame they aren't playing the *Liebestod*. Now then, if you two will just get on the bed. You know, I really feel quite like Petronius Arbiter. What a pity we haven't time to explore the possibilities of this piquant scene more fully. However, there isn't much time."

Maggie looked at me, I nodded and she got on the bed. There wasn't anything else for me to do but try to rush him. Maggie would have sense enough to run...at least I hoped she would.

"I think it would be most unwise of you to be heroic at this point, Timmy dear." He had to shout over the radio. "I shall get you both no matter what and it will just be unnecessarily messy. Now don't be difficult, Pet, I want to arrange you nice and pretty...at least as good a job as I did on Nellie. Still I'm afraid it would be impossible to make this look like an accident. However, I promise when they find you, you will go down in history as the romance of the ages."

This was the time. That miracle hadn't happened. Now or never. I got ready to jump. Well, I thought to myself, here goes nothing....

*"Robert, put down that gun."* It was a shout from the doorway. LeBranch quickly glanced over his shoulder. Backed by the superintendent, Mr. Frobisher was standing in the doorway. He had a gun in his hand and it was pointed at Le Branch.

"Go away. It's too late," yelled LeBranch. "Go away." He took one step nearer us. "Get on that bed," he shouted at me. His voice broke into a scream. *"Get on that bed!"* I didn't move.

"Robert. Put down that gun. We can work this out some way."

"It's too late for that." His fingers whitened at the knuckles. The pistol snout was pointed at my head. Frobisher moved toward us.

*"Robert!"*

I sprang at him.

The two explosions came almost together. A blinding flash...a force like a kick in the face...then blackness. That's all I remember.

It was quiet when I opened my eyes. Water was dripping on my face. A sharp ache seemed to be bursting my skull. I struggled to sit up. There were lights on. More blew up in my head.

"Lie still," said Maggie softly. "Lie still. You'll be all right, darling."

"But where is he? What happened?" She looked past me toward the floor. I rolled over on my side and squinted over the edge of the bed.

I had seen it before. In England, in France, in Germany, huddled figures holding their dead in their arms, rocking back and forth in stunned agony, crooning a wordless song…comforting a body past comfort.

Mr. Frobisher raised his head and looked at us. Tears were streaming from his browless eyes. His face was gray as death. Mechanically he was stroking the head he held in his lap. The ridiculous fur hat had fallen to one side and with it the black wig. The white face, the glistening, bloody mouth, contrasted grotesquely with the short brown hair. A frightening caricature of the face in the photograph on Frobisher's desk.

"He's dead," said Mr. Frobisher dazedly. "I killed him. I killed him."

"Bobby was Mr. Frobisher's son," Maggie whispered softly.

Mr. Frobisher heard her and his head snapped up.

"My son?" His tear-filled eyes hardened. "My son died in the war." He looked down at the body in his arms. "This is not my son. My son died in Normandy. Do you understand? He was killed in the war…not like this…. My son died in the war…."

# CHAPTER TWENTY-NINE

THE NEXT TWENTY-FOUR hours were just a blur of faces punctuated by exploding flashbulbs. Doctors' faces, policemen, detectives, city officials, Frobisher, Jo-Jo the rubber, Peters, Libby, Lieutenant Heffran…and they had even rounded up the basket man, the two soldiers and my Samaritan couple. I must have had my picture taken a hundred times, but a hell of a lot of good it did me now with my head all bandaged up like the Invisible Man's.

Oh yes, now I was the little hero. But what did I have to show for it? No job. My best suit covered with blood they'd probably never be able to get out—and a scar on my temple. How bad that was I wouldn't know till I could take off the bandage.

Well, Sunday's *Times* had better have a nice long help-wanted column. I might as well start getting my name down on lists. I hoped I hadn't completely forgotten how to work a bulldozer.

And as if that wasn't enough, Maggie up and announces she's flying to Mexico immediately.

Fine thing! That was gratitude for you. If it hadn't

been for me she wouldn't be alive today. But no...off she's going into the wild blue yonder.

I was going to tell her what I thought of her walking out on me when I needed her most and I would have, too, only I realized that when you came right down to it, if it hadn't been for me she wouldn't even have that bump on the back of her head, much less almost have been shot. Knowing that didn't make me feel any better, either.

But the final straw was when she even had the nerve to ask me over to help her pack.

I was sitting on the bed in her bedroom morosely watching her stuff things into grips. From time to time she would make me get up and sit on a grip that took all my hundred and eighty pounds to force shut.

"For Heaven's sake, Timmy, stop looking so disapproving and get us a drink. You promised me a belt from the office bottle, remember." I got the drinks and gave her hers and sat down on the bed again with mine.

"You are aware, I suppose," I said as nastily as I could, "that they have a limit on the amount of luggage a passenger is permitted to carry."

"Yes, dear. Quite aware. And do stop sulking. I know perfectly well you're furious because that bandage isn't photogenic, and you didn't get booked for a week of vaudeville."

"There's no need to be offensive."

"Well, is it my fault nobody gave you your little chance in front of a crackling fire to tidy up all the loose ends?" I didn't even deign to reply. "That is what's eating you, isn't it?"

"Partly," I admitted.

"Well, go on then."

"Of course, if you're not interested..."

"Oh, darling, I'm ecstatically interested, but I've got to finish packing. The plane leaves in an hour. Can't I listen while I pack? Do I have to sit openmouthed at your feet? Personally I think we were both dopes not to have figured out Bobby was a woman all along. I mean, there was the Pyramus and Thisbe reference in Kendall's letter...Thisbe was a man dressed as a woman. And you told me Libby said Vince Wagner had wanted Margo for Rosalind in *As You Like It* the moment she walked into rehearsal of that Equity library play thing...impersonation again and then lying about it to us in "21," and saying it was for Nora in *A Doll's House.* You were pretty stupid not to have caught on right away."

"Now wait a minute. Who's telling this story? You or me?" This wasn't at all the way I had planned it.

"But it's all so obvious. Nellie knew Bobby was Frobisher's son way back in *Front Page Stuff* when Bobby was a dancer in it and Frobisher was the stage manager. Frobisher wanted to keep an eye on him and sort of protect him from himself, and he even made Bobby take another name just for appearances. But in spite of everything Bobby started getting into scrapes, and instead of letting him eventually end up in prison, Frobisher thought he'd feel more at home in Hollywood where he could find a congenial little clique. All in all he had a fine time with his father paying him to keep out of his life and getting jobs dancing in movies to keep him amused."

"What a pity he didn't stay in Hollywood. He'd probably be a Goldwyn Girl by now. Where did you find out all this?"

"Oh, Bill told me," said Maggie.

"And who, may I ask, is Bill?"

"Bill Heffran. You know, Lieutenant Heffran."

"Oh, so now it's Bill, is it?"

"Well, darling, I had to talk to someone while you were so busy hogging the cameras." She had found another pair of shoes in the bottom of her closet, which necessitated opening a grip and trying to close it again. Even both of us jumping on it wasn't enough so she said to hell with it and threw them under the bed.

"What else did dear Bill tell you while you were getting so chummy?"

"Well, let's see, Bobby came back to New York when the war started to keep out of the draft because he dressed more or less like a man out there. Here, he always passed as a woman."

"Except, of course, when he was killing people."

"Oh, that's what Bill calls a 'double bluff' because Bobby was at heart a transvestite, whatever that means. I forgot to ask Bill...."

"I can see how you would be busy with other things."

"Don't be petty. Anyhow, Bobby had been helling around town always as a woman and appearing as a man was a disguise because it wasn't what he was most of the time, which was what he wasn't... Oh nuts, you know what I mean."

"Too bad the army didn't catch up with him then...with his pants on."

"You know, Frobisher's the one I can't help feeling a little sorry for. Imagine being so disgusted and ashamed of your own son that you told everyone he had been killed in the war rather than admit he was your son."

"Did Bill also tell you how much of all this Frobisher knew?"

"Oh, Bobby kept his father posted on everything, even boasted about it. He had him over a barrel because Frobisher had also been paying Nellie blackmail. But to give the devil his due, I do think he would have confessed or made Bobby confess if the police hadn't so obligingly announced that Nellie died of heart failure. Of course, Bill knew all along that it wasn't an accident."

"Oh he did, did he?"

"Yes, they could tell at the autopsy the way the spindle went in or something. They let it get in the papers that it was an accident to lull the murderer into a false sense of security, he says. He says that if you'd told him all the truth at the very beginning you could have saved yourself a lot of unpleasantness."

"That's damn sweet of Bill, I must say. I suppose he'll get promoted now?"

"As a matter of fact I think he already has been."

"Bully for him, the big slob. Did he tell you how Bobby knew I had the Youth and Beauty Book in the first place?"

"Oh, yes, Frobisher told Bobby. He guessed from the way you shot your mouth off in Sardi's. And he figured that if he and Bobby could get that and destroy it, what with the murder being called an accident, they'd be safe. That's the only reason he cast us in the show. To keep an eye on us and find out how much we knew. Really, when I think of how you forced that understudy business on Bobby when he only came around to the theater to see how you were making out after he and Jo-Jo bungled killing you the night before. No wonder Frobisher wouldn't speak to him. Really, you were an ass."

"That understudy was Libby's idea, not mine. But ass or not, young lady, you're still alive." I didn't mean to say that. It was unfair, but I was getting mad.

"Oh, Timmy." She dropped the clothes she was holding and ran over to the bed and threw her arms around me. "Don't think I'm not terribly grateful and you were ever so brave. Honestly you were. But you'll have to admit you were a damn fool all the same."

I had to admit that.

"Well, I guess I certainly tidied up all the loose ends all right, all right," she said. "And don't be unhappy. Bill said that for an actor you had an awful lot of nerve, but please next time you find a corpse just pick up the phone and dial 0. It will save a lot of trouble all the way around."

"I guess he's right. But tell him for me there's not going to be a next time. You meet such unpleasant people.

One Bobby is enough. How do people manage to mess themselves up like that? How wrong can you get?"

"I guess he just couldn't quite kiss his elbow."

"Now that's a bright remark. What's it mean?"

"What? You never heard that saying when you were a kid?"

"Certainly not. What utter nonsense. Kiss whose elbow?"

"Such a dull childhood you must have had. Why your own elbow of course. When I was a little girl I wanted terribly to be a boy and they used to tease me by telling me if I kissed my elbow I'd turn into one. Or if you were a boy you'd turn into a girl. I tried and tried to kiss it but I could never quite reach it. I guess Bobby tried and tried, too, but he could never quite reach it, either." I started, like a dope to try it. Maggie grabbed my arm. "No, Timmy, that's the whole point—it's physically impossible. But don't even try, I like you the way you are."

"So I gathered, mousing around with Lieutenant Heffran, stealing all my thunder about loose ends and now buckety-buckety off to Mexico." I stood up. Everything was flat, empty. I was tired. Tired of kidding myself. "You'd better hurry if you're going to catch that plane."

"Oh my God, yes. Help me get these things in a taxi, will you?"

What else could I do? It took three trips to get all the grips to the elevator and three more to get them out on the sidewalk. I flagged a cab and helped the driver spread them around. Maggie got in the back.

"Well, have a good time," I said sourly. "Send me a postcard when you hit Acapulco." The driver shifted gears and I started to close the door.

"Wait a minute, Driver," said Maggie. "Hop in, Tim."

"What for?" I didn't think I could face watching her plane take off.

"Oh," she said, "didn't I tell you?"

"Didn't you tell me what?"

"You're coming to Mexico with me."

"I'm *what?*"

"You're coming to Mexico with me."

"You're nuts. Go ahead, Driver." He shifted gears again.

"Wait a minute, Driver," called Maggie. "Don't be difficult, Tim. It's all arranged. I've got the tickets and the reservations and everything. We can have a whirl. Hop in."

"You must be out of your mind. I can't do it, Maggie. Go on, Driver."

The driver clashed the gears again.

"Wait a minute, driver," said Maggie.

"Now look, lady," said the driver. "Fun's fun, but nobody wants to get hysterical. Are you going or aren't you?"

"Your flag's down, isn't it?" said Maggie, regarding him hotly.

"Yes, lady, but…"

"And your little meter is working, isn't it?"

"Yes, lady, but…"

"Then relax." The driver sighed and picked up a tabloid from the seat and unfolded it over his face and leaned back and went to sleep. "Now, then, Timmy, if you're worried about clothes and things, we can buy anything you need. It's your reward for saving my life."

"It isn't that, Maggie. It's... I don't know but I just can't."

"Give me one good reason."

"There's hundreds, but, Maggie, why do you have to go?"

"Give me one good reason why I should stay." There wasn't one, now that Operation Hollywood was a complete bust. If I'd gotten that start—and I almost had...almost...opening night—I was going to give her one good reason for staying...a long, long time... But now...

"I guess there isn't any. Goodbye, Maggie." I wanted to kiss her goodbye more than anything else in the world, but I knew if I did I wouldn't ever leave her. And I knew that I had to now.

"You're sure you won't change your mind?"

"I'm sorry, Maggie, but I can't."

"I think I knew all along that you wouldn't."

"Maggie..." I hesitated.

"Yes, Tim?" she said eagerly.

"Maggie, do you like bulldozers?"

"Why, of course, I'm mad about them. What are they?"

"Never mind," I said. I realized it was hopeless.

"Oh, dear. Did I say the wrong thing? I'm sure I

could grow to love them if I only knew what they were."
I tried to smile. "I did say the wrong thing, didn't I?"

"No. I'm afraid you said the right thing." I slammed
the door. "Goodbye, my darling." I leaned in the open
front window to wake up the driver. I pulled the tabloid
off his face and he woke up and sleepily started to shift
gears again, but something on the front page caught my
eye. "Hey, wait a minute."

"Aw, mister, have a heart."

"Let me see that paper." I grabbed it through the
window and looked at the front page. My hands began
to shake. "Hey, Maggie, look." I opened the door and
jumped in beside her. "Look at this." I started to get
excited. "My picture's on the front page. My picture,
right on the front page. See?" And there it was. Right
next to a woman who had shot her whole family, including the dog.

"Let me see," said Maggie and snatched it from me.
She read the caption aloud. "Actor Traps Fiend. Story on
page three." To hell with the story on page three. What I
couldn't get over was the photograph. It wasn't one with
bandages. They had dug up one of the Trindler glamor-
puss ones and even as a newspaper cut it looked fine.

"Listen, Timmy.... Listen to what it says...." And she
read the story aloud. There were other pictures, even
Maggie's, other names and marking spots but I got top
billing. Me! Operation Hollywood hadn't failed after
all. It had only gone through a strategic withdrawal and
was starting up again. The show wasn't postponed, the

paper said. Miss Randall was going to take it over, and it would open in Wilmington as scheduled.

"Oh, Timmy, I think it's wonderful."

"Wonderful. Hell, it's perfect. Don't you see what this means.... I've got that start...a little publicity...it's what I've been praying for."

"I think it's fine."

"Maggie, you're not going to Mexico. Don't you see there's a reason now?"

"Oh, you mean because the show is opening?"

"Guess again."

"I can't imagine."

"We're going to get married."

"Well, it's about time."

"You mean you don't mind?"

"Oh, Timmy, you fool. I'd practically given up. There's just so much a girl can do."

"Good. That's settled, then. But it's not going to be easy."

"You're telling *me?*"

"There are a couple of conditions."

"I was afraid of that."

"One...we live on my money."

"I think that's wonderful. Have you got any?"

"Well, maybe not right now, but don't you see what this means... Maybe movie offers... I'm rich.... At least I'll have a hundred and twenty-five bucks a week in the show."

"Don't boast, Timmy. So'll I. But do we have to live in that dreadful Casbah?"

"Yes, until we can find anything better that I can afford."

"Please can I buy my own clothes?"

"Well…"

"You can pick them out," she said hurriedly.

"Well, temporarily," I said magnanimously, "but only temporarily. Is it a deal?"

"Ya got me, pal. It's a deal." I kissed her for sixty-five cents on the meter.

"Maggie," I said suddenly.

"Mmm-hmm?"

"We better call up and cancel those tickets." You have to pay attention to those things when you start having responsibilities.

"Maggie. Look at me." She looked at me and I had trouble remembering what I was going to say. "Maggie, I'm not so sure you ever had any tickets for Mexico at all."

"You know, Timmy," said Maggie, "I'm not so sure, but I think you're right."

# HARLEQUIN®
## VINTAGE
## COLLECTION™

# I'LL BURY MY DEAD

## James Hadley Chase

"This is a personal matter. Someone killed my brother. I don't like that. If the police can't take care of it, then I'll bury my own dead."

Nick English meant every word, but his efforts to find his brother's killer started a chain reaction of murder and violence that nearly ended his own life.

**Available now for a limited time only!**

**COLLECT ALL SIX ORIGINAL NOVELS FROM HARLEQUIN'S EARLIEST YEARS!**

**www.eHarlequin.com**

# HARLEQUIN®
## VINTAGE
### COLLECTION™

**PERRY LINDSAY**

Terry McLean was Phyllis Gordon's first and only lover;
moreover, Terry really loved her. Phyllis had rid herself
of her unrequited passion for her millionaire employer,
Kenyon Rutledge. And Kenyon's fiancée, Letty Lawrence,
was also well equipped with beauty and brains.

The arrival of Phyllis's little country cousin, Anice Mayhew,
spelled danger for both Phyllis and Letty. For Anice was
dewy-eyed and diabolically innocent.

### Available now for a limited time only!

### COLLECT ALL SIX ORIGINAL NOVELS
### FROM HARLEQUIN'S EARLIEST YEARS!

**www.eHarlequin.com**

VCNNG

# HARLEQUIN®
## VINTAGE
### COLLECTION™

# PARDON
## my
# BODY

**DALE BOGARD**

From the moment Dale's headlights hit the nyloned legs of lovely Julia Casson on that old Connecticut highway, trouble moved right in on him—and stayed there.

Gunmen, straight coppers and crooked coppers, luscious bedtime lovelies and the fabulous mystery of the Task Force dagger deaths… Bogard cracks his way through it all to the most breathless showdown ever.

### Available now for a limited time only!

### COLLECT ALL SIX ORIGINAL NOVELS
### FROM HARLEQUIN'S EARLIEST YEARS!

**www.eHarlequin.com**

# HARLEQUIN®
## VINTAGE
### COLLECTION™

## YOU
## NEVER KNOW
## with WOMEN
### JAMES HADLEY CHASE

Veda Rux steals a priceless Cellini dagger from the safe in millionaire Lindsay Brett's home. Floyd Jackson, a private investigator and first-rate blackmailer, asks her to return the dagger before the theft is discovered. But, blinded by the beauty of Veda, and by money, he agrees to her proposition. From the moment he fell in love with Veda, his doom was sealed, and he was caught up in a relentless intrigue that makes him a cat's-paw for murder.

**Available now for a limited time only!**

**COLLECT ALL SIX ORIGINAL NOVELS
FROM HARLEQUIN'S EARLIEST YEARS!**

www.eHarlequin.com